# THE WEST STREET HAUNTING

## Donald Smyth

ISBN-13: 9798306941448
ISBN-10: 1477123456

Cover design by: Brandi Doanne McCann
Library of Congress Control Number: 2018675309
Printed in the United States of America

*To Christine, Samantha, Jane and especially Mom*
*(Because she would have loved this book!)*

## Prologue

I'm just going to say it. The problem of immediacy that evening as dusk raced towards its ultimate and decisive rendezvous with total and complete darkness, my feet tapping in uncomfortable rhythm beneath the picnic table at which I was seated, cursing the fact that the pool house didn't have a bathroom the whole time, was that I needed to pee. And I needed to pee *bad!!!*

"I'll go in if you go in," I said hopefully, to Nog, my companion in this mutual circumstance of misery.

"I'm not going in until they get home," he stated decisively.

"Come on, man," I tried again.

"No," he said, putting an end to my attempt to take a whiz by employing the tried and true strategy of approaching a problem by securing the advantage of having safety in numbers.

I shouldn't have been surprised by his reticence, and I probably wasn't, but that made the outcome no less disappointing, as I looked across the parking area to the second floor of the darkened apartment where I wanted to take refuge from both the mosquitoes and the relentless urging of my overfilled bladder. Not to mention the fact that we hadn't had anything to eat or drink since having lunch, about seven hours earlier. To be fair, Nog had flatly refused to even come here for the longest time. His sister and my brother married two years prior, and they occupied the apartment in question. But Nog had not visited them for six months, not since the house's dirty little secret had convinced him that seeing his sister this way, in this particular setting, was an idea best worth avoiding.

It all started on a cold night back in February, with an innocuous post-midnight trip to the bathroom. Everyone was asleep but Nog, who had gotten out of bed in the middle of the night and navigated his way through the darkened house to the bathroom, where he promptly shut the door and took a seat on the only throne that mattered in that particular room. Suddenly, unexpectedly and without warning, the door flew open as if someone were about to rush in and intrude upon the private moment, the chandelier hanging above the dining room table, just outside the bathroom door began to shake violently, accompanied by all of the dishes sitting in a strainer alongside the kitchen sink and the pots and pans beneath, causing a ruckus in the room that sat off to the left and on the other side of the bathroom wall. He had not previously been privy to the fact that the place was haunted, and it was a terrifying introduction to the house's long and sordid history of ghostly encounters. And until I came to visit my brother and his wife that July, he had flatly declined the opportunity to return. He and I had struck up a friendship two years prior, so he'd made an exception this one time. But even now, he still wouldn't enter the house without an adult present.

The afternoon of that August day had seen my brother and Nog's sister leave to go to a wedding at around one o'clock in the afternoon. Seemed like no big deal at the time, there was a family pool out back and Nog and I planned on a day of hanging out by the water, swimming and what not. It kinda sounded like it might be fun to have no adults around, and I'm sure that it was. For a little while, anyway. But having an adult around was eventually going to prove to be important. The ultimate problem for us that day is the fact that weddings can take a long time to get from A to Z. First you've got to drive to and then sit through the ceremony. Then you have to drive to and attend the reception. And then you have to drive back home again once you're all partied out. What Nog and I didn't plan on was the fact that as 8:30 approached, that we'd still be sitting poolside, the novelty of which had long since been worn down to a dull nub by that point, courtesy of the incessant and numerous biting insects, stomachs that hadn't been fed since lunch and bladders that hadn't been emptied within that same timeframe. We both wanted to go inside in the worst of ways. But the problem keeping us both poolside was the fact that even though no one was home, Nog and I both knew that the house wasn't unoccupied.

'Screw it!' I thought, in a moment of false bravado. If I can't get Nog to go inside with me, I'll just go myself.

The house was a colonial style home with three floors, housing two apartments on the first floor and one large apartment on the second, capped by a full standing attic that was unoccupied and used for storage. My grandmother had lived in one of the two downstairs apartments, but she had passed away about five months earlier. My cousin lived in the adjacent apartment, but he wasn't home. If anyone living had been in the house at all, then it wouldn't have been a problem, but as it was, I decided to strike out on my own and make a break for the upstairs bathroom. My target was the first room on the right as you entered the apartment through the kitchen, about a dozen feet from the front door. It wasn't very far from the entrance and I didn't plan on staying a second longer than was necessary to complete the task. Certainly, I could at least do that much. Couldn't I?

"I'm going in," I announced, hoping that my initiative would spark a similar response in Nog. Maybe he just needed to see that I was serious, but it didn't work. He didn't budge a wink.

The walk across the parking lot was the easy part, but even that had the headwinds of ultimate doubt working against it. The apprehension was already building in my chest as I climbed the concrete stoop leading to the front door, and continued as I dragged my reluctant self up the stairs to the second floor, plugging away one heavy step at a time. Standing outside the door to the apartment, I hesitated while looking down at the handle. Then I reached for it, gave it a twist to the right and stepped inside. Immediately, I flicked on the kitchen light, which was the only light on in the entire house. Standing just a few feet inside the door, which I deliberately left wide open in order to facilitate a hasty retreat should it become necessary, I made the mistake of hesitating. I should have just made a beeline to the bathroom. But instead I stood there, looking out across the darkened dining room that sat adjacent from where I was, stifling my breath so that I could listen closely to every sound that the house was making. The bathroom was one room over and to the right. Just a few feet away in distance, but from here to the moon in my mind. All was quiet, but I already knew that I wasn't alone. I could sense it, and the heavy feeling of dread was as palpable as standing beneath a wet blanket. I turned around and left the kitchen without taking another step towards the reason why I had come in the first place. Bladder relief would have to wait. What's a few more hours of discomfort worth anyways? At least I wouldn't be risking an unwanted encounter with the supernatural. Been there, done that. I wasn't interested in a repeat. Even if it meant waiting until midnight. Or longer, if necessary.

C hapter 1: First Encounter

I was eleven years old the first time that I saw the ghosts. Actually, I never did *see* the ghosts. It's more accurate to say that I both saw and heard what they did. It started out innocently enough, on what seemed to be nothing more than just your run of the mill, average, ordinary summer day. I lived in Florida at the time, but soon after the start of school summer vacation in June of 1979, my mom brought my brother and I along with her as she headed north to babysit my cousin's infant daughter while my mom's niece and her husband went away on a week-long vacation.

I knew nothing about the haunting at the time. These weren't stories that were passed around at family gatherings for the sake of amusement. The things that were happening, and had been happening for decades, were real, unnerving and not suitable for open discussion, especially with children. In fact, the subject of ghosts was never talked about around any of us kids for fear that it would frighten us, even though anyone who spent any amount of significant time in the house was bound to find out for themselves that something odd was going on. I mean, it's not like the milkman was necessarily going to see something while making a delivery (and yes, there really was a milkman dressed in white who delivered milk in glass bottles to my grandmother's front stoop every week), but it was like I was told several years later by someone who lived there, "something happened almost every night."

The funny thing about my first time was that it didn't even happen in the house that everyone talked about as being haunted. My cousin lived in a similarly styled home right next door to my grandmother, the houses being no more than twenty feet apart from each other, separated by only a single driveway. That particular morning, my mom had decided to take a trip to the local grocery store, a place then known as Eddie's Supermarket. A neighborhood friend had come over to play, so I was allowed to stay home alone with her while my mom and younger brother went shopping. There was a pool table in the attic, and we ended up going up there to play. Around noontime, I asked Leah if she wanted to go downstairs to get something to eat. She agreed and we left the attic. But not before I'd racked the balls, rested the pool sticks against the frame to the door and turned off the light. We ended up being downstairs for about half an hour. Around twelve-thirty in the afternoon we started climbing the stairs to the attic to resume playing, heading up the first set of stairs to the second floor and continuing to the left, past the door to the second floor apartment before starting our ascent up the second set of stairs leading to the attic. There was still nobody else home at this point, at least nobody that would qualify as *living.* The room housing the pool table sat adjacent to the staircase. I was about a quarter of the way up when I noticed that the light to the pool room was on. I didn't say anything, but my mind started to wonder.

'*I could have sworn that I shut the light off,*' I kept thinking.

I puzzled over the question of what I was seeing, vs what I thought that I remembered. Then we stepped foot in the room and it got even weirder. The rack that I had left seated over the balls was resting on the near-side edge of the pool table. The balls had been broken and both cue sticks were laying on the table.

"Didn't we..." I said, as we both stopped dead in our tracks upon entering the room.

"Yeah," said Leah, without letting me finish.

"Let's get out of here," I said, as we both turned to the stairs and hustled our way back to the first floor.

I don't remember much after that. As I write this, it happened forty-five years ago. I vaguely recall that we just sat in the living room and waited for my mom to return from the grocery store. I imagine that we were both like, *what the heck just happened?* I do remember my mom carrying in the groceries. Did I tell her what happened? Or did I keep it to myself, thinking that she wouldn't believe me? I don't remember. But it became obvious to me in later years that she already knew about the ghosts. Of course she did. She grew up on West Street.

How could she not?

C hapter 2: Second Verse, Same as the First

It wasn't any less scary the second time something happened to me. In fact, it was much worse. A year later in 1980, we were back in Massachusetts visiting with family and staying at my grandmother's house. It was a ritual which had repeated itself in our experience for all long as I could remember at that point. Every summer, my mom took us kids north to Massachusetts to visit with family. But this time was a little different. This time, my mom's older sister was dying of lung cancer. She lived in the second floor apartment, above where my grandmother lived. The same apartment that I would so desperately want to enter three years later when I had to pee so badly as I sat out by the pool, waiting for someone to come home. It was a somber reason for visiting, to be sure. But in a lot of ways for a twelve year old kid, it was business as usual.

I think that it is fair to say that I didn't have any experience with death prior to that occasion. I had never personally known anyone who passed away, nor had I ever been intimately familiar with someone suffering from a terminal illness. I had never been given any reason to give the subject any real thought or consideration. To that point in my life, I had never even had a pet pass away on me. I had no real understanding of what it meant in terms of impact. It is also true that I had probably never considered as a consequence of that fortunate resume the possibility of what came after. Sure, my mom took us to church, and that offered a fantastical explanation for what comes after life. But how did that account for what had happened to me the year prior, when I'd left the pool room in my cousin's attic, only to return a half hour later to find that someone in the otherwise empty house had been playing pool in my absence. That summer, as my aunt passed away in June and her husband followed in July, both inside of that second floor apartment, I was about to get a deeper understanding about death and what comes later, courtesy of yet another encounter in that very same pool room.

This time I was by myself. Maybe it was because of all of the sadness swirling around the situation regarding my aunt's imminent demise or otherwise, it was true that summer that the pool room on the third floor of my cousin's house had become a popular spot for a coterie of similar minded people to hang out, shoot pool, joke around and smoke cigarettes. That's why it didn't set off any warning bells one afternoon when I was walking the driveway between the two houses and heard laughter and jumbled conversation pouring forth through the open window of the third floor attic. I could also hear the telltale snaps and cracks of cues and billiard balls striking and bumping into each other.

'*Cool!*' I thought to myself. '*Everybody is hanging out in the pool room.*'

Without giving it a second thought, I headed for the attic to join in on the fun. I loved playing pool and I liked hanging out with the assortment of family and friends that frequently gathered there to play. I had nothing to do otherwise, I'd just been walking around aimless and bored with myself, welcoming with open arms and excitement the opportunity to do something more interesting than that. Little did I know.

After entering through the front door, I was immediately met by the staircase climbing to the second floor. This led to the door to the second floor apartment. Turning left, I headed down the hall before turning left again to the landing of the second set of stairs leading to the attic. I was two or three steps into my ascent when I heard the cue ball take a hit and then strike some combination of balls. Everything seemed copacetic to my expectations at this point. In fact, it was exactly what I would have expected, given what I'd heard from the driveway. The light to the pool room was on. I could see that as I climbed higher, and there were distinct sounds of a game in process coming from the room that sat directly in front of the stairwell that I was now climbing. Then I got the feeling that something wasn't quite right. In opposition to the party atmosphere vibes that I'd been getting from the driveway, everything had gotten strangely quiet. When I got to the top of the stairs and entered the room, I was surprised to find that it was empty. There was every indication that someone (or something) had been playing, but there was no one around.

At first, I got mad. My first impression was that everyone had hidden themselves when they heard me coming because they didn't want me around. But I quickly denounced that idea. For one thing, you couldn't possibly leave the pool room without being seen from the stairwell that sat directly across from the door in question. From the driveway, I'd heard an eruption of laughter that implicated the presence of numerous individuals. I'd been almost half-way up the stairs when I heard someone take a shot. Was I now to believe that a group of people had scampered out of the room directly in front of my line of view without me seeing a thing, or hearing the scuffling of bodies in motion or feet pressing into the hardwood floor, in what would have been a mad dash to concealment? To be certain, I poked my head out into the hallway and looked left and right, my heart sinking deep inside my chest as a chill put goose flesh to my skin and literally raised the hair on the back of my neck. I knew what the truth was right then and there. I was the only living person in that attic, and I knew it intuitively. There was no place to hide in the sparsely filled attic, even if you wanted to. As anyone who has ever been in the presence of ghosts for real can tell you, there is a pervasive and distinct feeling that you get that you are not alone that stands in stark contrast to what your eyes and ears are telling you. Call it a 'sixth sense' if you need to do so in order to understand it better. That inescapable feeling that you are being watched by something that you can not see. I had that feeling, big time. And it was frightening. In desperation, I looked out the attic window to the adjacent attic window to my grandmother's house, wondering if I had misinterpreted where the sound had been coming from. After all, there was a pool table in that attic as well. But the window to my grandmother's attic was closed. I hadn't been wrong about what I'd heard or where it was coming from, and I knew it. With as much composure as I could muster, I calmly removed myself from the room and headed down the first set of stairs, as if nothing at all were amiss. Then I jumped down the last four stairs to the landing and flew down the second stairwell before running out the front door as fast as my feet would carry me. I had probably never been so scared in my life. But I was about to make the same mistake.

Three days later I did the exact same thing. I'd been innocently passing between the two houses when I once again heard the sounds of a gathering coming from the open window to the third floor attic. Again I was enthralled by the opportunity to hang out with friends and family, giving no consideration whatsoever to what had just happened to me a few days prior. Once again, I climbed the first set of stairs and then the second set before announcing my arrival to a room full of nothingness. My heart sank immediately. My skin chilled as if put to ice.

*'I can't believe that I fell for it again!'* I thought.

I couldn't fathom in that moment how I could have been so stupid as to let it happen twice. But the reality is that such encounters are unnatural to the average person's way of thinking. It is not normal to hear the sounds associated with a room full of people playing pool, to stop and ask yourself if there are actually people playing pool and hanging out or if they're ghosts. It only becomes a real question in the most extreme cases of circumstance and life experience. It's arcane and unfathomable. And no one ever does that. Even though I probably and obviously should have.

I would later learn that I wasn't the only one to have an unnerving experience in the driveway separating my cousin's house from my grandmother's. One afternoon as my sister was passing through that spot, she heard our aunt call her name. Even though she had already passed away. On another occasion, as she and a friend sat in my grandmother's attic gossiping and reading teen magazines they heard someone climbing the stairs. When no one came in, they went to look. No one was there.

Despite having a couple of encounters with empty rooms on my part, there were also few occasions where I was hanging out in my cousin's attic with real people when something strange and unusual happened. On one occasion, I heard someone coming up the stairs to the attic. When I poked my head out of the pool room to see who it was, there was no one there. The stairwell was empty. When I walked back into the pool room my older brother confronted me.

"Who was that?" he asked me.

"I don't know," I replied. "There's no one there."

On a different afternoon, when I climbed the stairs to find actual people playing pool, I took a seat in one of the metal chairs lined up against the wall so that I could watch. Right away I noticed something resting on the floor, laying between the legs of the chair I was sitting in. I reached down and picked it up. It was a hand-written letter dating back to the 1890's. The paper was old and yellow. It contained a message written out in cursive, in a language that I didn't recognize but was probably Swedish. There are two reasons why I think that. First of all, the town in question was a popular destination for Swedish immigrants in the early to middle part of the twentieth century. Secondly, the family that my cousin purchased the house and property from were of Swedish descent. As far as the letter was concerned, provenance provided a plausible reason for why it might have been in the house in the first place, but it didn't explain how it got beneath the chair, and if I hadn't had those previous encounters with the pool playing ghosts, then I wouldn't have given that notion a second thought. But the weird thing about it was that it hadn't been there before. I would have noticed it. People hung out in that room on an almost daily basis and no one had ever seen it before.

"Where did you find this?" someone asked me.

"It was just sitting right there, under the chair," I said.

The chair that I'd been sitting in was the kind of seat that you might expect to find parked behind an overhead projector, and if you went to school back in '70's or '80's then you know exactly what I'm talking about. Every school library had one. It had an orange pad each for the seat and a matching one for the backrest, screwed into a metal frame with four legs and no skirt. The letter had been placed on the floor, beneath the seat as if someone (or something) had been sitting in the chair reading it, and then casually bent over to put it down and tuck it away, possibly in a hurry as if having been interrupted. Knowing what I know, I believe that it belonged to one of the ghosts that frequented the attic. I think the spirit had been sitting in that very chair, reading it and probably reminiscing about some aspect of its life when it realized that someone was coming. With no time to stash it away, the letter got deposited beneath the seat where I later found it. Seems to be a reasonable assertion, given the age of the letter, the fact that no one had ever seen it before (including the owners of the house) and the fact that numerous supernatural occurrences were definitely taking place in that room at the time that the letter was discovered.

What ended up happening to the letter?

I don't know. Someone took it downstairs and I never saw it or heard another word about it again. But I would like to think that it found its way back to the attic, and whoever or whatever had left it there beneath the seat in the first place.

Chapter 3: It's off to Grandmother's House We Go

It is worth noting right off the top that my grandmother's house is only 8.7 miles away from the famous Conjuring House in Burrillville, Rhode Island. A short 14 minute drive away. That didn't seem very significant when I began working on this project, but it's going to be important later. I was told by a longtime resident that the house was built in 1910, but records list the date of build as 1840. The house was a colonial style build originally, with a rectangular facade, central front entrance and symmetrically placed windows. The exterior was made of wooden clapboard siding when I was a kid, although the structure looks significantly different today than it did forty or fifty years ago. One feature that set it apart from your standard colonial style home was the addition of two wings attached to each corner on the backside of the house, giving it the shape of a staple if you were to look down upon it from directly above. The wings, which housed a stairwell each, added a laundry room to the second floor as you looked at the house from behind, and a kitchen to the first floor apartment. The right wing added a kitchen to both the upstairs apartment and also to the smaller downstairs apartment, one floor below.

"Those additions were rumored to have been salvaged from an old house that had been torn down," I was told. "You can tell the difference by looking at the wood in the basement. The wood under the additions is much older. It's not the same," he said.

If it's true that the wings on the back of the house were salvaged from a much older home, that may explain the disparity regarding the date of build. It's possible that the main house dated to 1910 but that the additions were from a house built in 1840. It makes sense, but I'm not sure where the truth lies.

My grandmother, who was born in 1904, bought the house in the 1920's and lived there with an assortment of relatives until her death in 1983. I never once heard her talk about the place being haunted. But I know that she knew. Each day, the windows facing the old rail bed would begin to shake violently at one o'clock in the afternoon. At the exact same time that the Boston & Hartford train used to pass by the house. Only the train had ceased running past the house in 1955 and the ties were long gone. For decades after the fact, the house still rumbled to the schedule of the train passing by. It always frightened the children in the house, to which she would explain that it was because water was running over a nearby dam. There was no nearby dam. She knew the place was haunted. She would joke about it to others. Then again, like I said before, the situation regarding the comings and goings of ghosts was never discussed around us kids. So that may be the reason why I never heard her talk about it. It wasn't until you saw something yourself that you were let in on the secret, because at that point, the cat was already out of the bag.

Why, how and when the ghosts moved in is a mystery that is difficult to pinpoint. In researching this book I heard a suggestion that there was an Indian burial ground nearby, and even though there is an old burial ground not far from the property, I don't buy it as an explanation for the haunting. For one thing, there is no tangible evidence that the house itself sits on sacred ground. Another reason that it doesn't work for me is that the presence of the "dreaded Indian burial ground" is a common and overused trope in fiction conveniently deployed to explain the occurrence of a haunting, see *The Poltergeist* as an example of that cop-out excuse of a catalyst.

Ancient Indian burial grounds are a far too common trope in fiction, used to explain the reason behind a particular haunting. In real life, this abandoned cemetery from the early to mid 1800's is about a mile from the West Street location. It is so old that most of the stones are illegible. In back are a set of seven stones from one family who all died only months apart in the 1830's, from mother to father and children ranging down to only a few months old. Did tragedies like this curse the land around it?

Another common reason given as a possible explanation for the occurrence of a haunting is land or property, including specific buildings or houses, that have been exposed to significant amounts of bloodshed or death in the past, particularly when the violence was extreme, brutal and unexpected. An example of this kind of haunting would be the Gettysburg battlefield area, said to be one of the most haunted places in Pennsylvania. Or, the Pennsylvania State Penitentiary in Philadelphia, another supposed hotbed of ghostly activity.

Also implicated as the catalyst for a haunting are houses where murders are said to have taken place, such as the Lizzie Borden house in Fall River, currently a Bed and Breakfast that books out two years in advance and also serves as a museum, courtesy of the "forty whacks" that she gave her father with an ax back in the early part of August in 1892 (maybe she was just crazy from the heat, given all of the layers that women were forced to wear in the nineteenth century).

The house on West Street sits on land originally inhabited by the Nipmuc tribe. European settlement of the area began in 1662, so it's possible that the area saw its fair share of blood stained soil, given Massachusetts' penchant for Indian wars and all of the butchery that took place between those two opposing groups as they fought over who owned what in the seventeenth, eighteenth and nineteenth centuries. Not to mention what might have occurred in the area during the revolutionary war. The problem is that there is no historical documentation showing that any conflict took place on this specific stretch of land. The house itself however, did have a bit of a dark past that we can verify as accurate and true. For example, prior to my grandmother buying it in the 1920's, the house had been used to hold wakes, with the dead bodies being laid out for viewing in the front bedroom of the downstairs apartment. It is also factual that numerous people took their last breath in the house. Although these were of natural occurrence and none as the result of murder and violence. Whatever the source of the haunting was, it is absolutely true that the house in question saw many dead bodies pass in and out through the front door.

A third explanation that was floated to me is the belief that water is a medium between the spiritual and the real world, and that ghosts can use water as a conduit for manifestation. In order to drain water from the train tracks behind the house, a culvert ran the length of the rail bed as it passed through town. This culvert had drain points that allowed the water to empty all the way down to the Blackstone River. One of those ditches sat in the backyard of my grandmother's house, the drain of which passed beneath the yard, ran under the driveway separating my grandmother's house from the house next door, and across West Street all the way over to a barn on Snow Street, where yet another ditch opened up to catch runoff, before continuing down to the river. Each ditch had a grate that was susceptible to clogging, and this would cause my grandmother's backyard to flood out terribly in the years before a second drainage system was installed to prevent it.

Additionally, it has been speculated that an underground river might pass directly beneath the property. But whether this is true or not, what seems to be fact is that at different points in its history, a significant amount of water has passed beneath the property that the house sits on.

So that offers some possible explanations for the *how* and *why*, but what about the *when?* The oldest story corroborating the existence of a haunting on West Street dates back to the 1950's, and an incident involving my grandfather and his night nurse.

Sometime in the years immediately following WWII, my grandfather's health began to deteriorate due to some undiagnosed ailment that my mother would later blame on Parkinson's disease. By the time the 1950's rolled around, he was wheelchair bound and unable to care for himself. This necessitated the need for around the clock care that was too much for one person to handle. In order to be able to sleep at night, after taking care of my grandfather all day, my grandmother hired a visiting nurse to care for his needs while she slept. It did not end well. As the story goes, she took off in the middle of the night, running down West Street and screaming as she left the house. When contacted the next day, she informed my grandmother that the place was "too haunted" and that she would not be coming back.

Some years later, the unexplained noises the house was making was evidently still causing problems for the people who both lived, stayed and visited the house. One night when my parents were visiting, my father grabbed a hammer and climbed the stairs to the attic in search of an "intruder" that he believed had gotten into the house. They could hear footsteps on the ceiling of the second floor apartment, as the sound of someone walking back and forth across the attic floor filtered down from the space above, leading them to believe that someone had broken into the house, since no one was supposed to be up there, and everyone else who was known to be home was awake and accounted for. Not surprisingly, when he got to the attic, my father found no evidence that anyone had been up there, even though they had all distinctly heard it otherwise.

"The attic was the source of a lot of activity," I was later told by one longtime resident. "You could always hear someone walking around up there. Some nights it got really loud."

It seemed to be one of the common themes to the haunting, but that wasn't the most interesting part of it. There were many times when it was possible to catch a glimpse of what or whom had been making all of the noise.

"It wasn't unusual," I was told, "to be outside in the parking area and look up to see someone looking out the attic window. It happened all the time."

One resident who lived in the infamous second floor apartment from 1981-1985 told me that the activity was particularly bad in the years following the deaths of my aunt and uncle in that very same apartment in 1980, suggesting that maybe the occurrence of recent deaths had somehow been a catalyst to further happenings. He also told me that it had gradually declined in frequency from an occurrence happening virtually every single night all the way down to stopping entirely by the time they moved out. A later interview that I had with a more recent tenant disagreed with that assessment.

"The hauntings never stopped," he told me, as he proceeded to recount some of the scariest and most terrifying stories that I had ever heard about the place. This is what he and others who experienced similar encounters had to tell me about their time at the house on West Street...

C hapter 4: What Richard Experienced

Of all the people that I spoke with and interviewed in preparation for telling this story, no one knew more about or had more life experiences regarding the house on West Street than Richard did, having been raised in that infamous second floor apartment and then spending over fifty years of his life calling it home. In fact, Richard and his family had spent so much time there, that the feeling of a "comfortable arrangement" seemed to have developed between the living and the dead.

"They didn't hurt you," he told me. "I wasn't bothered by it." At least not until it became obvious to the ghostly part of this living arrangement that Richard and his family were planning on moving out. Then it lashed out, perhaps in frustration over the prospect and uncertainty of a change in roommates.

One night, as Richard was getting ready for bed, after a long and extended day of working on his new house and getting it ready for the family to move in, he watched as an entity stormed in from the bedroom window and raced along the ceiling, knocking a clock off the wall and nick-nacks from a bureau before circling the room three or four times and exiting through the door, where it made its way to the bathroom and knocked a pair of folding closet doors to the floor after ripping them off their pivot brackets and dislodging them from the track.

"It wasn't an orb," he told me, when I asked for clarification. "It was like..." he paused, struggling to find the words to describe it, "a wave of energy. You could see it. It bent the air around it and distorted it, in the same way that heat bends light and makes things look wavy and blurry."

As he told me this story, I couldn't help but think back to December 1983, not long after Christmas had come and gone. At the time, my brother and his wife were still renting that second floor apartment. Just outside the master bedroom was a pool table, and one night I was in there shooting some balls around all by myself. Bending over the table to line up a shot, I looked up and noticed the bedroom window curtain directly in front of me blow with force as if taken to the ceiling by a strong gust of wind. It made me wonder. It was cold that night. Real cold. Cold and still outside. The kind of cold December night in New England where nothing is moving outside. It made no sense to me that the window would be open, but if a gust of wind hadn't moved the curtain so violently, then what did? I put the cue stick down on the table and determined that I needed to take a closer look. As I moved with trepidation to the master bedroom I wondered if I really wanted to know the answer. Standing in front of the window, with the curtain drawn across it, I couldn't tell if it was open or not. But I didn't feel the cold draft that I might have expected an open window to be giving off on such a frigid night. I hesitated at first, gathering my courage. Knowing that a closed window could probably only mean one other thing. Then I grabbed the curtain and pulled it aside.

Shut!

I couldn't breathe at first, for fear of what that meant. Then I noticed that one of the panes was broken. I let go a sigh of tepid relief. That seemed to be the answer for what I had witnessed. But what about the storm window?

Being from the Florida Keys, I didn't understand the concept of double-hung windows, with a storm window seated behind it. We didn't have those down there. Every house that I had ever lived in had windows that crank out, and because of the way that those windows opened, there were no storm windows behind them. Although, many of them did have metal shutters attached to a track that was itself attached to the house, separate from the windows themselves.

But in New England, most houses had storm windows. The house on West Street had storm windows, and that made sense because no one would just leave a broken window subject to the cold of winter like that. You wouldn't be able to efficiently heat a room that way. Owing to the bliss of my ignorance, I was willing to blame the movement of the curtain on the missing pane. In retrospect, I'm not so sure. To this day, I don't know why the curtain blew to the ceiling that night. But it was the same window that Richard saw the entity come through some thirty years later. As for me, I turned around and returned to the living room so that I could be in the company of other people.

Game over.

Coincidence or not, the second floor door to the attic was in that bedroom, with the hall and stairway directly on the other side of the bedroom wall. The window in question was the closest one to that wall.

For Richard, witnessing the entity come through the window was an unusual show of aggression by the spirit involved. But it wasn't the first time that it had shown displeasure at something. Years earlier, their young daughter had been up in the attic playing by herself when she took a scratch to the back by an entity that was apparently angry that the young girl was moving things around and taking pictures off of the wall. Most of the time, the encounters were more benign than that. For several years, he told me, there was a female apparition that would appear at the foot of the daughter's bed almost every night, silently looking down at the young girl as she slept, as if she were keeping watch.

"She had on an old-time dress," he said. "It was white and bulbous from the waist down," he added, describing a style of dress that would have been popular sometime in the middle to latter part of the nineteenth century.

"Could you see her face?" I asked.

"Not really," he said. "The features were kind of indistinct."

Given the predictability of the manifestation, I wondered if he had ever taken a picture of it.

"I tried. They never came out," he replied. "It was just a blur."

He also set up time-lapse cameras and video recorders, to no avail. What he usually ended up with was blurry, blotched and indistinct wispy images, if he managed to catch anything at all, suggesting in part that maybe the energy used to manifest a haunting doesn't lend itself to being captured by the technology of standard photography. Still, it made me wonder if there was a way to capture a clean, unadulterated image of a ghost on film, so I approached an expert.

"We didn't use any special cameras when we were out on an investigation," said Amie Simard, a retired lead investigator with the paranormal investigation team ParaPatrol, operating out of Gardner, Massachusetts. "Our only consideration was the use of red flashlights," she added, explaining how the red beam produced enough visible light to aid most cameras lacking night vision capability, while allowing the investigator to maintain a low and unobtrusive profile.

My next question for Richard was more pertinent. Had he ever been fearful for his daughter's safety?

"Not really. The apparition never bothered anyone," he explained. "She just stood there, floating at the foot of the bed," looking down at his daughter as she slept. "I kind of liked it. I thought it was interesting."

More unsettling than interesting was the time that he witnessed a shadowy figure sitting on the sloped roof of one of the additions.

"It was about three or four feet tall, dark and shadowy, sitting on the edge of the sloped roof, looking right at me. It had red eyes," he told me, reminiscent of the demons that reputedly inhabited a house just two streets over in the 1970's. Richard, who had gone to school with the two boys who lived in that particular house would listen knowingly as his schoolmates recounted the things that were going on in the home.

"They had demons," he told me. "Demons! They had to leave the house on two separate occasions."

Aside from the manifestations and various noises that came from the attic, just as strange was the distinct smell of coffee being brewed every morning. The problem of which was the fact that nobody in the house drank coffee.

"We didn't even have a coffee pot," Richard told me. "Nobody drank it. But every morning you could smell it brewing in the kitchen."

The scent of strange things in the air with no corporal association to account for its presence was not a new thing, nor was it specific to Richard's experience. Many years earlier, my mom had told me a story about waking up every morning to the smell of coffee brewing and burnt toast. When she mentioned it to someone, she was told that it was just a dead uncle still going about his daily routine.

Even though they weren't brewing coffee, the family did enjoy hosting parties. And every time they did, the ghosts would make an appearance.

"You could see them all standing in a back corner of the room, from the corner of your eye, every time we had people over for a gathering. It was like they wanted to be a part of the celebration."

In the years leading up to the Covid lockdown, Richard and his family finally moved out of the second floor apartment on West Street for reasons unrelated to the haunting. Initially, some of the paranormal activity followed them to their newly built home, as if attached either to the living beings themselves or to the things that had been relocated in the move, such as furniture, personal items, keepsakes and mementos. However the spirits somehow managed to hitchhike to the new house, according to Richard this activity ultimately proved to be sparse and ephemeral when compared to West Street, stopping altogether in a relatively short period of time after making a brief appearance. Today, Richard lives relatively ghost-free with his family, for one of the first times in his entire life.

C hapter 5: What Brenda Experienced

Brenda knew something about what she was getting herself into in the middle of the 1980's when she moved into the second floor apartment to be with Richard, her significant other at the time and future husband. At the very least, she couldn't say that she hadn't been warned about the situation.

"I learned about it beforehand," she admitted. "I had heard about it from different members of the family who would talk about all the sounds the house was making and the different things that were happening there."

So, what did she think of all of the hype?

"When I heard the stories, I didn't believe they were true," she admits candidly.

For Brenda, the transformation from skeptic to true-believer began when she started seeing and hearing things for herself.

"I would hear footsteps in the attic, and the sound of someone walking around. Sometimes it sounded like someone was moving furniture. So I went upstairs. There was no one there and no evidence that anything had been moved about."

And then there was the man in the hat. Like Richard, she also began to see something lurking about in their daughter's bedroom. Richard had converted the old laundry room to a bedroom for the young girl, and that bedroom door sat directly across from their own, with just an open common area between them.

"There was one time when I thought she was awake and still up in her bedroom watching us as we laid in bed watching television. That's when I would see him. He would be standing alongside her bureau, watching her as she slept."

"What did he look like?" I asked.

"There were actually two of them. The one in the bedroom had a crew cut. Sometimes he would be wearing a hat. You could see his face, but it was kind of indistinct at the same time. He was tall, probably six-feet, one-inch. The other one was slender, looked to be about five-feet, eight-inches tall. He had short, curly hair."

"What were they wearing?" I asked.

"They were wearing modern clothes," Brenda answered.

"What about the hat? What kind of hat was he wearing?"

"It looked like a fedora," she said.

The fedora is a hat with a soft brim and indented crown, that was first introduced in the 1890's, but reached its peak in popularity during the 1920's. It experienced a resurgence in the 1940's and '50's thanks to its placement in noir films of the era. This popularity lasted until the late 1950's, when the spread of less formal dressing became more mainstream. Taking into account the spirit's "modern attire," his crew-cut and his fedora, we can reasonably conclude that this particular ghost may have passed away sometime between the earlier part of the 1950's to the middle part of the 1960's. But who was he and did he have a tie to the house?

My grandmother owned the house and lived there with relatives occupying all three apartments. Had he been one of my mom's uncles? Or can any ghost manifest in a place unrelated to what they knew in life, simply because a portal exists that lets them do so? My mom may have been able to identify the spirit, if she was still alive. But unfortunately, she died during the Covid lockdown.

When she shared this story with her sister-in-law, who lived in the larger apartment just one floor below, she learned that the woman's own young daughter was also being watched over by a nightly visitor. Only this was an image of someone that they knew. It was recognized as the ghost of grandma Ruth, who had died in the upstairs apartment just a few years earlier.

Although they each reported seeing different things to me at different times, given to the fact of their mutual cohabitation, it only made sense that several of their encounters were similar to what the other had seen. For instance, Richard had seen a shadow person sitting on the edge of the roof, staring at him. Brenda had also seen a shadow figure, leaning up against the pool house outer wall. When she shouted to it, it didn't move. She'd also seen the angry entity storm through their bedroom window, and knock things off the wall as it proceeded to move room to room before leaving the bathroom closet doors laying flat on the bathroom floor.

Even though the bedroom manifestations always happened after 10 pm, and the shadow people even later than that, usually sometime after midnight, there was a shadow in one corner of the dining room that could frequently be seen from the corner of the eye as you passed through at all different times of the day. When they moved a few streets over just a few short years ago, Richard had confirmed to me that some activity had followed them to the new address, an assessment that Brenda shared as well.

"I think we have something here," she said of the new place. "Once in a while I think that I see something in the living room from the corner of my eye. I can feel their presence. One day it's going to catch me off guard and I'm going to scream."

C hapter 6: What Terri and Alan Experienced

When she said "I do" in the spring of 1980, little did she suspect that those nuptials would result within one year's time a move to a certain second floor apartment of particular infamy. She had to know. The stories were a not so well-kept family secret amongst the inner circle by this point, with the activity spiking in intensity and frequency following the recent deaths in that apartment by the prior tenants, serving as the catalyst for the reason why it was available to rent in the first place.

"No one ever told us anything about the place being haunted," Terri acknowledged, recalling the events forty-three years after moving to West Street, and thirty-nine years after she moved away. "Everything just started happening."

That "everything" she referred to began much the same way that her younger brother Nog would find out about the situation some months later, with pots and pan rattling in the kitchen for no apparent reason. It was an occurrence that happened on more than one occasion and was observed by Alan and Terri both separately and together. But strange as that was in its own right, it may have had a reasonable explanation, if you consider it in a vacuum, that is. There have been approximately 410 earthquakes registering at least a 2.5 on the Richter scale in Massachusetts over the last 356 years. One of those tremors could have accounted for the unexplained shaking in the kitchen cabinets. Harder to explain away would be the things that happened after that.

It has long been a subject of speculation that both children and animals are more capable of seeing ghosts than adults are. Children, as it is said, have the advantage of an open mind at their disposal, while animals are gifted with a superior set of senses. The truth is, a dog's eyes work differently than a humans. Dog's have rod-dominated retinas that allow them to see better in the dark. If you have ever been outside at night and noticed the light from a dim star in your peripheral vision, that you can't see when you look directly at it, then you have experienced in some small way the difference between how a dog's eyes perceive the world versus your own.

The rods in the human eye are primarily located on the periphery of the retina and the cones (the cells used to detect color) are concentrated in the middle part known as the fovea centralis. That is why you can see some objects out of the corner of your eye, when you're mostly using your rods to see, but not see it at all when you are looking directly at it and depending upon your cones to see the same thing. In other words, it is a scientific fact that dogs can see things that humans cannot see as readily, if at all.

"I saw it out of the corner of my eye."

How many times have you heard this said in reference to a haunting? My guess is more than once. In fact, you're going to hear that a bunch as you read this book! And there is probably a good reason for that.

Humans see light at the lower end of the visible spectrum, having longer wavelengths running from about 450nm all the way up to 750nm. Dogs can pick up light a little lower on the visible spectrum, starting at 435nm. They can also only detect the colors blue and yellow, along with different shades of gray. Did you catch all that scientific mumbo jumbo? Because it's about to become important. This explains why dogs can see ghosts just fine, while humans usually only catch a glimpse of something "from the corner" of their eye, and lose it the moment they try to look at it directly. In all likelihood, it was probably still there. The difference is that the person went from using rods to detect it, to using cones when they looked directly at it. And as I just explained, the cones cannot necessarily detect what the rods can see. Tricky to think about. But we also need to consider that it's possible that supernatural manifestations may occur along different wavelengths in the visible spectrum at different times, since there are many cases where the apparition was seen clearly (as happened to Richard and Brenda on more than one occasion), and sometimes only the non-visual impression of a haunting is detected. In any event, an example of this phenomenon became apparent one afternoon as Alan and Terri sat in the living room of their second floor apartment in the company of their Samoyed, a dog named Jasper.

"Al and I were sitting in the living room," Terri recalled. "There was a large empty chair sitting adjacent to the couch, on the opposite wall, and all of a sudden, Jasper started barking incessantly at it. The hair on his back was standing up. We noticed that the chair had an indentation in the cushion, as if someone were sitting there."

As I listened to this story, it reminded me of a December morning back in 1983, where I had experienced a similar kind of encounter with the furniture in that room. My family was visiting West Street for the holidays and my younger brother and I, along with Terri's brother Nog, had been relegated to sleeping on the living room floor. There was a door between the living room and the adjoining dining room, which was closed and wedged shut with a newspaper that had been inserted between the door and the frame in order to keep it closed because the door handle didn't work. One morning, as we lay spread out like three little Indians beneath our covers, I heard the door handle rattle, as if someone had grabbed it from the other side. Then the door, which opened into the dining room, opened an inch or two and stayed that way for three or four seconds. All three of us turned to see who it was, as the newspaper sat still suspended against the frame. Then it fell to the floor and the door slowly swung fully open to reveal that no one was standing on the other side. The seat cushion on the chair just inside the door and to the left, sank as if someone that we couldn't see had just taken a seat in it. My brother, who was eleven years old at the time, got up and ran for the kitchen. Nog and I stood still, transfixed by fear and still laying on the floor.

Then Terri walked through the dining room.

"What?" she called out with sarcasm. "Are you guys too scared to stay in there by yourselves with the door closed?"

"We didn't open it!" we called out in unison.

There was only one way to get in or out of the living room, and that was to go past that chair. I determined right away that I wasn't going anywhere near it. At some point it became obvious that whatever it was had left.

As mentioned, children are said to be more sensitive to picking up the presence of a ghost than an adult would be. I've seen a host of reasons given as to why this phenomenon might be true ranging from the standard response of "children are more open-minded than adults, having a much greater sense of awareness to the things around them," to "they are better mediums of such energy due to the benevolence and purity of their souls." Culture and imagination have also been floated as explanations, pointing out that children raised in homes in which supernatural events are a topic of discussion may be more susceptible to the influence and development of such storytelling. One interesting hypothesis puts the blame on the pineal gland.

The pineal gland is a pine-cone shaped, endocrine structure tucked into the center of the brain, whose job it is to produce melatonin and regulate the sleep cycle, among other things. It is a light-receptive organ that is said to serve as something of a third eye to the body, allowing for a greater sense of awareness, particularly to "unseen light," or light occurring on the visible spectrum at a wavelength typically below what the average person can detect, not too dissimilar to what a dog can perceive, starting at 435nm. It is postulated that over time, calcification of the pineal gland (which can begin as young as two-years of age) reduces the ability to perceive this light, resulting in a return to the normal standard deviation in the human perception of visible light, sitting in the range between 450 to 750nm. This all makes total sense to me from a scientific perspective, and there may be some truth embedded in some or all of these explanations, but I personally wonder if the real reason why children are better at seeing ghosts isn't just because it's safer for the ghosts to show themselves that way.

Children have no clout, power or authority to effectively change the world in which they live. They can't bring in a priest to bless the house and chase away the spirits. They aren't going to call on a paranormal investigator. They aren't going to intrude or pry into an entity's personal business by holding a séance. To put it simply, young children aren't going to make trouble for the ghosts that show themselves. And they almost certainly won't be believed if they try telling an adult that they saw something. For years, my young daughter had an imaginary friend named Eddie the Ghost. I did my due diligence as a parent and asked her about him. But I never for one minute thought that she was actually referring to a real ghost. West Street, however? Now that was a totally different story.

One afternoon, as Alan and Terri were sitting in the company of visiting cousins at the kitchen table, they all chatted to the background noise of kids having fun rolling balls back and forth across the pool table, centered in the room that sat to the left of the dining room as you exited the kitchen. The children, all cousins ranging in age from three to seven, were enjoying themselves as kids do, "playing pool," whooping, hollering and having the kind of fun that only happens when you get kids together, while the adults talked and enjoyed each other's company two rooms over. Then someone noticed that the pool room had gone strangely quiet.

"We started to get up to check on them," Alan once told me. "But then they all appeared at the entrance to the kitchen."

"The ghosts are watching us play pool," said the oldest boy, still holding a pool hall in his hands.

"They all looked like they had seen something," said Alan. "Their eyes were as big as silver dollars. They all had a look on their face as if they had just done something wrong and expected to get into trouble for it."

Of course, when the adults went to look, the pool room was

empty. Young vs old pineal glands? A difference in the ability to perceive visible light? Open-mind vs adults set in their beliefs? Or just a case of active imagination. It's open to interpretation as to where the kids got the story from, but at least for Alan, he already knew that weird things were afoot in the pool room. He'd seen it for himself.

With his wife working third shift in the years coinciding with their move to West Street, Alan had taken the opportunity of coming into an inheritance to take some time off to work on his education. But this meant lonely nights spent alone in the upstairs apartment. To combat that feeling of isolation and loneliness, he took to a pattern of inviting friends and family over during the night to keep him company, drinking beer and shooting pool. One night, as he and his cousin John were doing just that, Terri arrived home the following morning to find them both sitting at the kitchen table.

"As soon as I walked in I knew that something was wrong," she told me. "I immediately asked what had happened. I swear that both of their faces were green."

As it turned out, during the night as they were playing pool, they both witnessed a long dress hanging in the laundry room move sideways as if caught by a breeze. The laundry room sat off to the left as you entered the pool room, with the master bedroom on the right and the guest bedroom directly ahead. The windows to the laundry room were closed. It wasn't near a vent or a fan that could have explained the sudden movement. It was as if someone had brushed past it while walking by. Chalking it up to *"what the heck was that?"* the two men resumed their game. Then John made an observation.

"I thought you said we were alone," he said to Alan, as he leaned against the wall opposite to and facing the laundry room, cue stick in hand and waiting on his turn.

"What are you talking about?" asked Alan, as he looked up from the table, leaning over and ready to take a shot. "We are alone."

"Well, I just saw a lady in a bathrobe walk across the laundry room!"

"All the blood just drained from his face," said Alan. "He just turned white."

For the rest of the night, the two men sat at the kitchen table, smoking cigarettes, drinking beer and waiting for Terri to come home. Thankfully, John agreed to stay.

"I don't think that I would have stayed there if he'd left," said Alan. And really, who could blame him.

Among the other phenomena that have some commonality when discussing the occurrence of a haunting is the prevalence of patterns in life that continue even after an individual has passed away. When I sat down to talk with Amie Simard, the retired paranormal investigator from ParaPatrol, she recounted details from an investigation centered around a town drunk.

"Every day he could be seen walking home from the package store with a case of beer under each arm." she said.

When he died, the family could still hear the sound of him falling down the stairs every morning at precisely three am. On West Street, similar things were happening.

On one particular afternoon, as Alan and Terri were sitting at the kitchen table talking with a cousin named Beverly, they all heard the sound of someone climbing up the stairs to the second floor apartment. When no one knocked or came in, Alan got up to open the door. No one was there. One hour later, at two o'clock in the afternoon, the kitchen door opened by itself.

"It coincided with when your uncle would come home for lunch," said Terri. "An hour later, it was like his lunch break was over and he was going back to work."

'Sarge' as he was called, was a retired military veteran who served as the town's postmaster right up until the day he passed away. Each day he would come home for lunch, which began at one pm and ended at two. A pattern that it would seem that he kept even in death. But coming and going for lunch wasn't the only impression that Sarge would leave on the apartment. A lifelong smoker, he suffered from an extreme case of emphysema, and the deep and deliberate wheezing sound that he made as he gasped for air could be heard throughout the house while he was still alive, a sound that numerous people claimed to have heard even after he died.

"I heard breathing when I was in your aunt and uncle's old bedroom," said Terri. "It sounded like it was coming from the attic space."

As if the sound of wheezing wasn't bad enough, it wasn't nearly as frightening as the time she felt someone place a hand upon her shoulder. When she turned to greet the feeling, there was no one behind her.

As for myself, I spent several weeks visiting with Alan and Terri in the summers of 1981 and 1983 when they were living on the second floor apartment at West Street and I didn't see or hear a single thing that made me wonder. True, I had already had some unnerving experiences with ghosts in the attic next door, but at my grandmother's house, where all of the action was supposed to be, my encounters were limited to the curtain blowing mysteriously in the master bedroom and the door to the living room opening by itself, both in December of 1983. But that didn't make sleeping there alone any less frightening for me as a kid. I knew the place was haunted. I'd heard the stories. Each night I set about trying to get Alan to stay up for as long as possible so that I wouldn't have to go to bed all alone, in the dark. That was the worst. When you couldn't see what was going on! Invariably, I never got him to stay up later than 3 am. Then I'd go to bed and lay on my back, staring at the ceiling so that I could try to see in every direction. Eventually, I'd fall asleep once dawn began to break and fill the room with enough light so that I could see that I was alone. It was scary stuff for a thirteen year old.

Unlike Richard, nothing seemed to follow Alan and Terri to their new apartment in Woonsocket, Rhode Island, when they moved from West Street in 1985. From that time forward, neither of them have ever had another run in with ghosts, the supernatural or anything else of the sort.

C hapter Interlude: A Ghostly Encounter? Or History Repeating Itself?

In giving consideration to the question of patterns followed in life being observed as continuing after someone has passed away, it is worth noting that there may be another explanation for such occurrences. As we just covered in the preceding chapter, the former tenant of that second-floor apartment on West Street seemed to be coming home for his lunch break even after he passed away, climbing the stairs at precisely one o'clock in the afternoon and then leaving one hour later. His distinctive wheezing could be heard in the house even after he passed away. The persistent smell of coffee brewing in an apartment with no coffee pot. Or ParaPatrol conducting an investigation where the town drunk could still be heard falling down his stairs at three o'clock every morning, after he had already died! But were these examples of ghosts continuing on with a daily routine in death? Or had those habits left an impression ingrained in the fabric of time, to be replayed long after it had happened by some naturally occurring phenomenon that we don't understand, allowing for images of some past event to be rebroadcast in real time as if it were happening again? It's an interesting question, and believe it or not, there is documented precedence for this kind of "haunting" taking place. Let's take a moment to talk about the Treasurer's House in York, Yorkshire, England.

Probably the best known, and most convincing, example of this kind of phantom encounter, involved an eighteen-year old heating engineer/plumber named Harry Martindale, who saw a Roman legion pass through the cellar of the Treasurer's House back in 1953, as he worked on repairing pipes related to a coal-fired heating system that was being moved by order of the National Trust (an organization dedicated to preserving the heritage of historic buildings and landmarks in England).

As he told the story frequently over the course of his lifetime, he was standing at the top of a ladder when he heard the sound of a trumpet giving off a series of short, quick notes coming from the space behind him, and growing louder as if the source of the musical progression was coming closer. As he turned around to meet the sound, he watched as a soldier wearing a plumed helmet emerged from the wall behind him and proceeded to march directly through his ladder, followed in short order by a cart horse and nine to ten pairs of legionnaires visible only from the knees up.

Terrified and falling from his ladder as a result, Martindale scurried into a corner to hide himself as he watched the "scruffy-looking" soldiers pass by and disappear into the opposing wall. He would later describe the legionnaires as sweaty and dirty looking, appearing as if they'd been marching all day along a dusty road. He claimed that they were dressed in green tunics having a tartan design and wore a round shield strapped to their left arm, accompanied by a short dagger-like sword, which was sheathed in scabbards attached to their right-hand side.

This description was immediately seized upon by skeptics who attempted to debunk his story by pointing out that there was no historical evidence to support his claim that the soldiers had been wearing green tunics with a tartan design on them. The round shields were also a problem for historians, because although they had been used in Rome, they were not believed to have ever been deployed for use in England, where only the large rectangular traditional shields of the Roman arsenal were thought to have been issued. Excavations of Hadrian's Wall would later prove conclusively, for the first time, that the Romans had indeed used round shields in England, a fact that Harry Martindale could not have known prior to his 1953 encounter. And green tartan tunics would also be discovered when an ancient Roman burial site was accidentally uncovered near a York train station. Something else that Martindale could not have possibly known, unless he had seen the fact for himself.

Further bolstering his claim, was the discovery of an ancient Roman road traversing through the property and leading to the ruins of ancient Roman headquarters. The paving stones of that road sat a mere eighteen inches beneath the floor of the cellar where Harry Martindale was working, explaining why the images that passed through the basement had only been visible from the knees up.

The fact the Martindale said that the phantom images were as solid as real people and didn't notice him, suggests that it was not a parade of ghosts that he watched march through the center of the cellar, but rather the replaying of an event that had occurred there centuries before, an image caught on the fabric of time and replayed as if someone had pushed the playback button on a video recorder.

Interestingly enough, Harry Martindale was not the first, or the last person to see Roman soldiers in the cellar of the Treasurer's House. An American professor is said to have been the first to witness the spectacle, back in the 1930's, followed by a curator, who had seen the manifestation seven years before Martindale fell from his ladder. Whether this represents the occurrence of an actual time slip or is merely the replaying of an image caught in space and time is debatable. But what we know for certain is that the phenomenon has not been exclusively limited to England alone. In fact, it has been reported as close to home as the Conjuring House in nearby Burrillville, Rhode Island.

I don't want to go too deep into what reportedly happened at the Conjuring House, because unlike the Harry Martindale story, where he described things previously unknown to academia but later proven to be accurate, the Conjuring House has a biased interest as a museum and money-making enterprise in spinning out stories to keep the ticket-buying public interested. But there is one particular story that I do want to mention because it ties in nicely to the type of phenomenon that I've been discussing in this chapter. It centers around a story involving Carolyn Perron, the matriarch of the family under whose proprietorship the events in the movie *The Conjuring* allegedly took place.

According to a story recounted by her daughter, Andrea Perron, Carolyn got up and left the parlor one evening to investigate voices that she could hear coming from the supposedly empty dining room. As she approached the threshold to the room in question, she saw that a large wooden table had taken the place of the family's own furniture. Seated at the table were an entire family preparing to have dinner. Nearby, a woman was cooking over a fireplace that had been sealed up for more than a century. As the strange woman, dressed in nineteenth-century attire directed some children to take a seat, a man who was already sitting at the table saw Carolyn Perron looking at them and stared her directly in the face. Then he elbowed the arm of the man seated beside him, and pointed the bewildered mother out before disappearing, with the dining room returning to its normal layout. What becomes obvious from the details of the story is that each party was aware of the other as each existed in their own moments in time, probably seeming as a ghost to the other's perspective. But this is not an example of a haunting, in as much as it was not a paranormal visit by long dead spirits. Rather, this is a perfect example of a time slip.

Now to be clear, these are not one for one comparisons. In the first example, Harry Martindale stated that the apparitions marched across the cellar floor and into the opposing wall completely oblivious to the modern world surrounding them. In the case of the Conjuring House, the nineteenth-century family did notice the intrusion. One is a time slip, and the other is merely a non-corporal rebroadcasting of an image imprinted on the fabric of time. But that is not the only difference between the two stories. The case involving the Treasurer's House is well-documented and backed up by evidence. This is unfortunately not so of the Conjuring House. You either believe the story or you don't.

If we consider both stories to be equally true, then we need to consider the possibility that all three supernatural occurrences may share a similar catalyst, since hauntings are sometimes reported concurrently in places where time slips or other images of past events have been witnessed. Indeed, although the Roman soldiers have been seen in the cellar of the Treasurer's House, ghosts have been reported in every room of that particular building. And the appearance of the nineteenth-century family having dinner in the dining room of the Conjuring House seems to match the description of a time slip and not a ghostly encounter. Although, it is certain that most of the paranormal activity tied to that location is of the haunting variety, based upon reputation alone.

Another thing to consider is that the overlap of activity may be the result of one phenomenon being mistaken for another. For example, a time slip for a haunting, and vice versa. But what set of circumstances would be favorable to allowing each, any or all of these supernatural occurrences to happen? At least in the case of the famous Bold Street in Liverpool, England, home to more reported time slips than anywhere else in the world, one hypothesis is the suggestion that electromagnetic energy given off by the city's underground rail network may have something to do with it. This again is backed up by scientific theory, since Einstein's theory of general relativity states in part that electromagnetic fields can have an effect on time and space, creating distortions and curvatures in the fabric of space-time. This however, does not explain the occurrences reported at the Conjuring House and observed on West Street, since no underground transportation exists in that area. But there is another explanation. Water.

Groundwater flows are known to increase the electrical conductivity of the surrounding earth. Ions moving in groundwater create friction, and this friction can create a weak electromagnetic field as it passes through different types of strata. This electromagnetic field is typically not of any consequence because it is so weak, but what if the strength of that electromagnetic field could be magnified significantly by the type of strata that it was passing through? Like quartz.

Quartz is a slightly magnetic crystal that is piezoelectric, containing both positive and negative charges. It has been suggested that quartz crystals at earth's core help to power its electromagnetic field. Is it possible that this is the explanation for the events that occur at West Street, the Conjuring House and numerous other unspecified locations? It's hard to know, but it is an interesting theory.

Back to time slips and the rebroadcasting of events lost to time. I like to equate the passing of time to music stored on a vinyl record. The Now is centered on the point of the needle as it passes through the grooves of a spinning record. This is your current living experience. But what happens to the moment that just passed? Does it simply cease to exist? Or is it stored in the fabric of time like the song in the grooves of a  record whose needle has already passed by? Is electromagnetic energy the force that distorts those grooves and moves the needle just so, allowing it to skip backwards, even momentarily? Is it also the force that allows portals to open between this world and the afterlife? Again, fascinating to ponder, and yet nearly impossible to prove, given to the fact that none of these phenomena are considered anything more to science than urban legends and bastards of an active imagination.

Chapter 7: What April Experienced

What appears to be true is that Sarge was awfully busy in the house, even after he died. But let's circle back to that. As the only girl, April was my grandmother's favorite as far she and her two siblings were concerned, spending each and every summer with her from the time that she was five years old or so. Back in the 1970's parents could walk a child to the gate, where an airline representative would take said child directly from the parent and bring him or her onboard the airplane. From there, the child would be seated in their assigned row and then be watched over by the flight crew. When the plane arrived at its destination, the whole process worked in reverse, with the child's guardian meeting them at the gate. None of this is possible anymore, but April did just this throughout the 1970's until she was old enough to fly on her own.

My grandmother lived in the smaller of the two downstairs apartments with her blind and mentally challenged brother, a sweetheart of a man named Harry. This was the same apartment where wakes had been held earlier in the century, back in what was now Harry's bedroom.

"I had a tangible sense of never being alone in Harry's room," April told me. "It always felt like there were other souls present. The temperature in that room was always colder than the rest of the apartment."

The small apartment in question had only two bedrooms, a living room and a small kitchen. Out front was a hallway leading to the front door, which was used as a pantry. To the left was a staircase leading to the second floor, which was sealed off at some point in the mid to late 1970's. My grandmother's bedroom sat adjacent to the living room and had an on-suite bathroom. But it is kind of generous to refer to it as such. It was really just a toilet and a sink that had been haphazardly added to the space and was separated from the rest of the room by a curtain. I hated using that bathroom. It felt like you had no privacy when you were attending to your business, since even the bedroom didn't have a door. And forget about going number two. You just sat there praying that you weren't going to let one rip to a chorus of laughter as you just tried to hurry through the process as quickly as you could. But I digress. As far as April was concerned, she would sleep in my grandmother's queen-sized bed as a little girl during these summer visits, and that would be the catalyst for the most interesting story that she had to share with me.

Sarge was an old army guy who got up with the sun even after his time in the armed services had passed. The house, which had not been plumbed until the 1960's, had plenty of exposed pipes, and each morning before he left for work he would tap on the pipes in the bathroom in order to wake my grandmother in the apartment below. Why she just didn't use an alarm clock like everybody else, I don't know. But this is the arrangement that they had. When he passed away in July of 1980, April recalled still hearing the distinctive tapping on the pipes even after he was gone, from the perspective of her spot in my grandmother's bed, each morning and every day after. As if nothing about the situation had changed. It was a narrative that fit in nicely with everything else that was going on at the time, since his distinctive emphysemic wheeze was reportedly heard by several different people both in the kitchen and in the space leading up to the attic long after he had passed away. And a phantom presence had been witnessed coming and going for lunch by no fewer than three different people between the hours of one pm and two in the afternoon. By the evidence taken from numerous eyewitness accounts, it seemed at least on the surface of things that Sarge had failed to move on. Did he not realize that he was dead? Or did he go about his usual routine because he didn't know what else to do with his new and current situation? *Did the presence of a strong electromagnetic field beneath the property open a portal between this world and the next, but block 'the light' that spirits typically follow to their next destination?* Or did it simply give them the opportunity to stay? Whatever the true answer to that question is, it is clear that Sarge wasn't the only spirit who decided to stick around. His wife was also making her presence known. Her name was Ruth.

One afternoon, as April was walking the driveway between the two houses, with my grandmother's house on the left and my cousin's house on the right, she heard Ruth call her name from above and behind. When she turned to confront the voice, there was no one there. This was the same driveway where I had heard the spirits laughing it up and playing pool in my cousin's attic just prior to or just after this happened. Although she couldn't be sure exactly where the voice had come from, it seemed as though it might have come from a second floor window, or possibly the attic window. Ruth's second floor bedroom had windows opening to that driveway, so that makes sense. Although the attic was also a possibility.

On another occasion, as April and her friend Jill were passing between the two houses together, they heard pool balls clashing and voices coming through the open attic window of our cousin's house. Just like I had done (twice!), they climbed the two sets of stairs to find that a game had been in progress, but no one was there to account for the noise that they had heard. Sometime later, while hanging out in my grandmother's attic together, reading teen magazines, gossiping and smoking cigarettes, they heard the distinct sound of someone coming up the stairs to the attic. Fearing that they might get in trouble, they stashed the magazines and swatted at the clouds of cigarette smoke to make it dissipate, but then no one entered the attic space. When they went to look, the stairwell was empty. Later still, while sitting in the parlor of that second floor apartment, she watched as the seat cushions of the couch deformed as if someone or something unseen had just taken a seat and was sitting there in her unknowing company. On one particularly frightening evening, the door to the living room opened to reveal Ruth standing on the other side, prompting the frightened occupants of that room to pull a blanket up over their heads and wait out the terrifying encounter beneath the cover of an impromptu and convenient hiding spot, effectively removing the manifestation from sight like an ostrich who buries its head in the sand. For some who were there that night. It would be the last straw. It would also be years before some of those who witnessed it would return to that second-floor apartment living room.

C hapter 8: What Wayne Experienced

As the younger brother of West Street Terri, Wayne quickly became one of Al's closest friends after he and Terri tied the knot in the spring of 1981. It was this social arrangement that provided the impetus for numerous trips to the second floor apartment on West Street that the newlyweds were now calling home. Unlike his younger brother Nog, who'd been initiated into the *House of Horrors club* while sitting on the porcelain throne in the middle of the night, Wayne had been let in on the secret from the very beginning, and before he'd had the opportunity to learn about it the hard way.

"I already knew about it," he admitted, when I asked him if he'd found out before or after he'd seen something for himself. "They told me all about what was going on."

"Did you believe the stories or were you skeptical about what they were telling you?"

"Yes, I believed them," he said. "I didn't have any reason to doubt what they were telling me."

Growing up in Burrillville, you would think that Wayne might have been presented with numerous opportunities to experience the supernatural before he'd ever stepped foot onto the West Street property, but that wasn't the case.

"We used to hang out in the area around the Conjuring House all the time," he said, "over on Round Top Road. Then we'd drive out to the lake to go drinking."

That "lake" was Little Round Top Pond and fishing area, a spot with its own dubious goings-on, and one which we will revisit later on in this book in the chapter on the old Arnold Estate.

"Did you ever see or hear anything strange in all your time living and hanging out in the Burrillville area?" I asked.

"No," he said. "But I wish that I had."

"Did you believe in ghosts prior to your first visit to West Street?"

"I had never been given any reason to think about it," he replied.

Not unlike myself, Wayne only had two occasions which left him scratching his head with wonder. The first involved the pool table, and the second happened in the kitchen. Both encounters would have sounded familiar to virtually anyone who'd spent any amount of time in the house, or even the one next door.

"I slept there on a couple of occasions," he recalled, "you could hear pool balls hitting each other in the middle of the night. It was weird, the house was dark and nobody was awake. There was nobody even playing pool."

One of the first things that Al had done upon moving to the second floor apartment was to buy himself a pool table. It was situated in a room in the middle of the apartment, to the left as you passed through the dining room, with the master bedroom to the right of the table and the guest room behind it. The laundry room sat to the left of the table. It was from his spot in the guest bedroom, behind the table that Wayne would hear the balls rolling around in the dark. On a different occasion, he'd heard the pots and pans rattling in the kitchen.

"Were you ever afraid or uncomfortable in the house?" I asked.

"No, I just thought that it was crazy," he said. "I'd never experienced anything like that before. It was crazy."

C hapter Interlude Part II : There Goes the Neighborhood

What became obvious to me as I researched this book was that the haunting on West Street is not an isolated incident, but more like one stop on a sort of ghost superhighway running through a specific stretch of Massachusetts and down into Rhode Island. Let's take a moment to talk about Julie's mom and the experiences that she has had living in a house just a few streets over from the Conjuring House.

For starters, Julie is related by marriage to West Street Terri, whom I interviewed back in chapter 6. I approached Julie and asked her if she had ever visited the second floor apartment at West Street, and if she had, did she ever see or hear anything weird during her time there?

"I'd been there a few times," she told me. "But I did not experience anything unusual myself. They told me a few stories about the place, but that's all that I know."

On the surface, it was a little disappointing. I was having trouble getting people to talk to me about their experiences there and I was hoping for a juicy interview. I wasn't surprised though. In all my time spent in that house visiting relatives during our summer family vacations, I myself had only had five distinct experiences that I would qualify as having no other explanation other than an encounter with the supernatural. It's not like stuff happened *all the time,* as in twenty-four hours a day. In fact, most of the time you couldn't tell that there was anything unusual going on. It was all about the timing. Even during that hotbed year of 1981, when I spent 4 straight weeks visiting my brother Alan and his wife Terri in that infamous second floor apartment, I didn't hear or see anything that would have made me suspicious. But I already knew that the place was haunted, so that didn't stop me from laying in bed at night, scared shitless and positioned on my back with my eyes trained on the ceiling so that I could see a little bit of everything with my peripheral vision, waiting for dawn to break so that I could finally close my eyes and get some sleep. To the house's credit, nothing happened while I was there that summer. To me, anyway. So I was disappointed that Julie had nothing to add to the house's dubious history, but not surprised. Then she threw me a curveball.

"My mom lives on Chapel Street in Harrisville, Rhode Island. A few streets away from the Conjuring House. Her house is supposed to be haunted," she told me. "I actually went to school with one of the girls who lived in the Conjuring House."

*What?*

"One of those ghost hunting shows did a segment on my mom's house. The woman who rents the basement apartment was told that there is a portal in her kitchen."

*'Wait a minute,'* I thought. *'There's more to this story than I bargained for.'* First West Street, then the Conjuring House, then demons a few streets over from my grandmother's old house. Now another haunting, down the road from the Conjuring house? *'There is no way that this is all just one giant coincidence.'*

"Oh, and my son LJ has also had quite a few supernatural experiences."

"Where does he live?" I asked.

"Two streets up from the post office where Alan and Terri lived," said Julie.

*'The post office down by West Street?'*

That's not only where Sarge spent most of his post military career working, it's like a 10 minute walk from my grandmother's house! Now I was certain that I was onto something. There had to be a common influence of cause that allowed all of these hauntings to be occurring in such a small radius of distance. But what?

"LJ and his friends had an experience in the attic where his friend lives," she added.

*'Attic?'* Of course they did. Where had I heard that before?

I had started this project with the intent of telling a story about my grandmother's old haunted house. But now it was clear to me that I needed to dig deeper than that. The real story was much bigger than I originally bargained for, and as far as I was concerned, they were all related.

"Tell me what happened at your mother's place..."

C hapter 9: Going to The Chapel and We're Going to Get Haunted

    The house on Chapel Street where Julie's mom lives also serves as Main Street for the town of Harrisville, Rhode Island. Like many small towns in New England, Harrisville is one of nine villages that comprise the larger town known collectively as Burrillville. It sits just 3.3 miles from the Conjuring House on Round Top Road, which is the actual geographical location of the famously haunted Arnold Estate, which served as the inspiration for the movie franchise. The house on Chapel Street was built in 1944, and is only 8.4 miles from the lesser known hauntings that have been observed both on West Street and other nearby locations in that town. The surrounding area was originally settled by Europeans around 1662, and originally belonged to the Nipmuc tribe. Like the house that my grandmother owned on West Street, the Chapel Street residence has three apartments accompanied by an unoccupied attic space. But unlike West Street, the Chapel Street house has been the location of several paranormal investigations, beginning in 2015, with a second investigator visiting the house one year later.

    Linda had been living in the basement apartment on Chapel Street for the last ten years, as of the time of this writing. It was her husband Tom who was responsible for initiating an investigation of the house, after the couple had borne witness to and been subjected to numerous unsettling and unexplained supernatural phenomena, occurring sporadically over the course of the first year or so of their time spent living at the home in question. For the record, Julie's mom lives on the first floor. Linda and Tom were her neighbors. Tom is now deceased, having passed away in 2020.

For Linda, her ghost problem began with the entity's apparent dislike for her cat Bear. A domestic shorthair with a smooth black coat, Bear liked to make himself comfortable in the family's living room recliner.

"Every time he laid down on the recliner, it started rocking by itself," recalled Linda. Making the startled cat jump down from it. "There were also two occasions when he was laying on the bed and then suddenly he's on the floor, like someone or something had pushed him off. I thought it was funny, but in a strange way."

Less humorous were the things that began happening at night.

"I got the feeling that someone was watching me when I would wake up in the middle of the night," said Linda. "Tom had to sleep in the recliner in the living room because he had respiratory problems. He had to sleep at an incline so he could breathe, so it made no sense that there would have been someone else in the room with me."

"WHO ARE YOU?" she shouted out one night in exasperation, as Tom rushed into the bedroom to see what was wrong.

"Nothing," she replied, since she hadn't actually seen anything. But that was about to change.

On one frightening occasion, She awoke to see a woman and two children standing at the foot of her bed, looking down at her and laughing. When she blinked, they disappeared.

"I had lots of experiences with those three," said Linda. "The females were wearing clothes from the 1800's, with bonnets and dresses that were very wide at the bottom (similar to the female apparition that stood guard at the foot of Richard's daughter's bed over on West Street). The boy was wearing some kind of outfit indicative of the same era. The girl was older, maybe seven. The boy looked to be about five."

She assumed that the woman was their mother, but wasn't certain how old she might have been.

"The woman wasn't always there," recalled Linda. "I had a

child's sized rocking chair in the living room, and I would see it rocking by itself. I also had dolls on a shelf, and I would find them on the living room floor as if someone had been playing with them. Tom had some matchbox cars, and he would find them in front of the couch as well."

Sometimes, it was the woman who seemed to appear without the children.

"There were numerous occasions where Tom felt something touch his forehead. I thought it might be the woman ghost kissing him, but he didn't think so."

On a separate occasion, she saw what appeared to be one of the ghosts petting Bear, as the sleek black cat lay sleeping on her bed. This was in stark contrast to the harassment that the family cat usually endured at the invisible hands of the spectral intruders. It was the second paranormal investigator to visit the house back in 2016 that informed Tom and Linda that they had an entity in their home that didn't like their cat.

"He was a friend of one of Tom's friends," recalled Linda. "He was a member of the production team for the show *Ghost Hunters.* Not a member of the original investigation team, but the guy who set up all the equipment they used to do the investigations."

So now they knew why the poor cat kept getting dumped on the floor, but that wasn't the only bad news that they received, as he also told them that they had a poltergeist on their hands, implying to the couple that it was "not not evil."

Back in 2015, the first paranormal investigator to visit the house at Tom and Linda's bequest determined that they had a portal in their pantry, and that this was how the spirits were coming and going from the property.

"He was also a friend of a friend," said Linda. "He had previously done an investigation at the Conjuring House."

While she couldn't remember his name, she did note that he was a well known paranormal investigator whose services were in high demand and that he had since moved to Australia.

"He came into the house with some kind of meter (probably

a KII electromagnetic field meter, specifically popularized by the show Ghost Hunters). I followed him into the pantry, where he said he was getting a reading. He was moving the meter up and down. This told him that there was a haunted portal nearby."

He went on to explain to the couple that ghosts get pulled into tunnels and then pushed out of the portal. Meaning that they could end up anywhere in the three-story house. He also told them that they could communicate with the spirits in the house by using a flashlight with an on/off button if they wanted to, a suggestion that Linda soon took him up on.

"I put the flashlight on my bed," she explained. "Then I asked it a series of questions. *Is there a spirit here? Turn the light on once for no and twice for yes.*"

The light flashed twice.

She then asked it a more poignant question: "*Are you going to hurt anyone in the house?*"

No, came the answer on one flash of the light resting upon the bed. It was a relief to the beleaguered housewife, but at the same time, that didn't mean that a variety of different entities were going to just stop using the portal to move from this world to that and then back again. Despite the intervention of two different paranormal investigations, the haunting continued unabated as both Tom and Linda began to hear the distinct sound of marching, echoing throughout the rooms of the basement apartment on a near nightly basis.

"I saw the back of a civil war soldier on several occasions, standing with a gun slung over his shoulder. He always had his back to me. I never saw his face. He was kind of foggy looking. Tom never saw him, but he did hear the sound of marching," Linda recounted. "I tried to get pictures of the ghosts on numerous occasions, but they never came out."

When asked if she had ever been made to feel unsafe in her home, she indicated that she had.

"There were two times that I was really afraid," said Linda. "And both times were in the bathroom."

The first incident occurred while she was in the process of

showering and something pulled the shower curtain open. The second time, she had just gotten out of the shower to find the word "Hi" scrawled across the steam-covered medicine cabinet mirror.

"That just really creeped me out," she said.

After that, her cat Bear was relegated to going into the bathroom with her when she needed to go. It was a strategic move that made perfect sense, since she already knew that at least one of the entities in the house didn't like cats. Although she was never certain about which ghost was following her into the shower.

Another phenomenon that was being observed at the Chapel Street residence was the failure of the recently deceased to definitively move on to the afterworld. And stay there. Back on West Street, and many years earlier, numerous people had reported seeing both Sarge and Ruth shortly after they had passed away. Now the same thing was happening over in nearby Harrisville. Only this time, the phenomenon wasn't being limited to just people, as one afternoon Tom approached Linda to say that he'd seen their recently deceased pet dog laying in front of the television.

"I didn't believe him at first," she recalled. Then one day she saw the dog for herself, walking down the hall as she exited the bathroom. When she called his name, he turned to look at her. Then he just disappeared. On a separate occasion, she entered the living room to see Bear's mother sitting on a shelf, next to an urn filled with her own ashes. When she called out to it, the mother cat jumped down and began running to her, before it too disappeared. Worst yet was what happened when Tom died in 2020.

"I saw him twice," confided Linda. "He was in his chair. The first time was about a week after he died. It was very vivid. I could see his clothing and he was wearing his glasses. I yelled out, *Tom! What are you doing here?* And he disappeared."

She still feels at times that she can sense his presence, as if he has hung around to make sure that she's okay. The interesting thing about it is that he even had the option to stick around at all. Just like West Street, we need to ask if following *the light* is even an option? Or is the electromagnetic energy that is allowing all of these manifestations to occur simply giving souls the option of hanging on to fragments of their prior life, even in death?

Another phenomenon characteristic of a haunting that was making the rounds at the Chapel Street house was the appearance of orbs. As it turns out, the very last encounter that Linda had prior to this interview in June of 2024 involved seeing an orb in her kitchen, next to the refrigerator.

"It was orange/yellowish in color and about the size of a softball," she said, in describing the encounter that preceded the appearance of yet another ghostly manifestation.

"Right after I saw the orb, a female ghost appeared at the sink. There was a man standing behind her, near the table. The woman ghost was wearing an apron over a dress and looked like she was washing dishes. The male ghost had an old-fashioned shirt on and some weird pants. I couldn't actually see their faces that well, but I could tell that the man had a waxed mustache (a trend that was popular in the United States back in the 1800's, particularly in the 1880's and 1890's)."

The very next day, she saw a similar orb in the kitchen. Soon after that, the couple were once again spotted standing by the kitchen table. When she asked them who they were, they both looked at her and disappeared into thin air. When asked if she had ever seen any other orbs, she admitted that she had.

"There were two other times," she said. "Once, I was going up the outside stairs to go check the mail and I saw an orb that was about the size of a baseball come out of a window on the second floor apartment and fly directly into the shed sitting next to the deck."

The other time, she saw an orb about the same size as the first, as it came out of the laundry room that abuts her apartment. It just disappeared after making a brief appearance.

Apart from the ghostly visits, the weird goings on, the flying orbs and the taunting of her cat, Linda has also needed to contend with the frustration of having things go missing, Back in 2015 and '16, the paranormal investigators who visited the house each warned her about the "Borrowers." Borrowers are a type of ghost that takes things and then brings them back. Sometimes the borrowed item gets put back in the same spot that it was taken from, and sometimes it isn't.

"There was one time when Tom insisted that he put his missing keys on the table when he came home, and they ended up in another location," recalled Linda. "There were other times that things went missing and then they returned."

On one occasion, when she went to the pantry to get a jar of peanut butter, she removed the lid and peeled back the seal to find the container nearly empty.

"I know that it was full when I bought it," insisted Linda.

Seems reasonable to believe her when she says that it was full when she bought it. It would be hard not to realize that there was something wrong if you picked up a nearly empty jar of peanut butter in the store. The absence of weight would be a dead giveaway.

"I could actually see where it had been scooped out," she added.

At the time of this interview, she'd had a book missing for four days.

"I told them to bring it back because I wasn't finished reading it," she said with a smile.

Inspired by all of the strange events happening all around her and motivated to get some answers, Linda undertook an investigation of her own by doing a little research into the house's background as well as the surrounding property. A trip to the Burrillville Library didn't turn up any information of particular interest, but she did uncover an article about a nearby saloon where people had been killed. It was interesting, but at the same time, when I started digging into the haunted history of the house on West Street, my first thoughts centered on what might have happened to that house and property that would have facilitated the accompanying haunting. And the answer appears to be *nothing!* With as many as five houses on West Street, two on Hope Street, five on or near Main Street, one on Chesley Street, another on Chapel Street, Ironstone Street, Preston Street, Miller Street, Center Street and three more on Chestnut Hill Road, that is not a coincidence, that is a pattern. It is definitely not house or property specific. And even though it's bad for business, that goes double for the Conjuring House as well. Sorry to be the bearer of bad news, but what happened at that location has nothing to do with Bathsheba Sherman or anyone else. Turns out that the Conjuring House is just one of at least two dozen haunted houses in the same general area. It just happens to be the one with a movie franchise behind it.

Scuttled by her attempt to dig up information at the library, Linda's next move was to talk to someone who had lived in the house, but had since moved away. This prior tenant had lived on the second floor, one apartment above Julie's mom and two above Linda herself.

"She told me that although she had never seen the civil war soldier in her apartment, she had heard what she thought was the distinct sound of a soldier marching," said Linda, "accompanied by the sound of drums playing in the unfinished attic. The kind of drums that would be played during a military march."

The woman also said that she had heard the sound of horses outside the three-story house at one point, but saw none when she looked outside. Given the history of the area, it is more than probable that military exercises had taken place either where the house currently sits today or on land that is very near by. During the American Civil War, there was virtually no corner of New England that did not supply troops to the Union Army, and Harrisville was no exception. Were those particular sights and sounds reported at the Chapel Street house part of the broader haunting that was taking place? Or just flashback images of a military drill or procession that had taken place on Main Street more than a hundred and fifty years earlier, in the exact same way that Roman soldiers could still occasionally be seen marching through the basement of the Treasurer's House over in England?

She'd also seen an American Indian crouching down by one of her chairs as she exited the bathroom.

"He appeared to be looking for something," the woman told Linda. "And then he just disappeared."

Once again, a ghost? Or just the image of a past event being rebroadcast in time as if it were happening now? Not so easy to tell. But one dead giveaway may be that ghosts respond to current and contemporary stimuli. While flashback images are oblivious to their modern placement in time, as they go about their business marching, or looking for things. The other major difference of course is that ghosts are dead, while flashback images are neither dead or alive. They are merely snapshots of something that happened once. Like a picture.

The woman had also mentioned to Linda how she'd once had a big, heavy shelf in her bedroom come crashing down for no apparent reason. Shoddy craftsmanship, or something more mischievous than that?

It reminded me of a story about West Street. When I was a kid, before I knew that the place was haunted, I fell down the stairs leading from the second floor apartment to the first. One moment I was going down the stairs and the next, I was sitting on the second step from the bottom wondering what the heck had just happened. It was weird and confusing. I had no memory of tumbling down the stairs or of even having stumbled in the first place. It was as if one moment had seamlessly moved to the next with nothing in between. To this day, it is the one and only time in my life that I actually fell down a flight of stairs. And I probably did. But because of what I know about my grandmother's old place, I have to at least ask the question. *Did I really fall down the stairs or was I pushed?* And that's the problem with haunted places. You're never really certain what you just experienced.

C hapter 10: Mom Knows Best, And Apparently Some Ghosts As Well

The experiences that Julie's mom has had at the Chapel Street address aren't all that different from what others have reported seeing and hearing at the residence in question. Just like my grandmother's house on West Street, it probably isn't possible to spend any real time there over and above what the occasional visit constitutes and not realize that something otherworldly is going on. Just like her downstairs neighbor, she has seen things, heard things, had things go missing, been taunted in the shower and had her cats terrorized. She has seen things moving from the corner of her eye and been made to feel afraid. This is what she had to say about her time living on the first floor apartment:

1) Although she hasn't seen him, she has heard the soldier marching.
2) Her cats have been taunted and harassed by an unseen entity.
3) She's had the "borrowers" take things and not put them back where they were.
4) She's seen the ghost boy and the cat.
5) She's been locked in her own shower and trapped in the bathroom.

Let's dig into the details of what she had to say.

Back in 2016, it was the investigator associated with the show *Ghost Hunters* that first told her neighbor Linda that there was an entity in the house that did not like cats. Julie's mom also has several cats, and these felines have not been immune to the same kind of harassment that their basement counterpart has experienced.

"There are times when they come running into the living room as if they are being chased," she said. "And I actually see them looking back at something. But nothing's there. I tell the ghosts to stop doing that," she added. "It's not very nice."

The female cat, she observed, stopped sleeping on the twin bed in the guest room, choosing to lay on the floor instead, despite the fact that she had been using the bed for years (was it because she kept getting pushed down from it?).

"I think that she got scared off of it," she said. "Sometimes they appear to be staring at something, but there's nothing to see."

Like both of her neighbors, Julie's mom has also heard the distinct sound of a soldier marching. Although, unlike Linda, she has never actually seen him.

"Sometimes I catch something moving through the apartment from the corner of my eye," she noted. "But it's never there when I look. I did wake up one time though, in the middle of the night, to see a boy staring me in the face."

Was it the same five year old boy that Linda had seen in her own bedroom on numerous occasions? Could be, but there's no way to tell from the information that I was given. She hadn't seen him long enough to provide a description.

"When I blinked, he was just gone," she added.

She has also seen a ghost cat running through the apartment on different occasions, but whether this is Bear's mom is also uncertain. How many ghost cats can there really be running around the place?

Like Linda, Julie's mom finds things on the floor with no real explanation for how it got there.

"I've had my jewelry end up on the bedroom floor," she said. "I know that from where I put it that it couldn't have just fallen off of the dresser."

Could it maybe have been one of her cats being curious? Could be. Cats love to knock things off of high places with their paws, there's no question about that. The problem is that when you have a confirmed haunting, there's just no way to tell. Was Bear the one leaving Tom's matchbox cars on the living room floor? I doubt it. But it is not just jewelry that has been found left scattered about. She has also found her phone and remote controls on the floor as well.

Scariest of all is what happened in the bathroom.

"My mom was in the shower," said Julie, "and she couldn't open the sliding glass door. It was as if someone was holding it shut on her."

Once she got out of the shower, Julie's mom then contacted the landlord and asked him to come over and inspect it.

"They came over and checked it out," said Julie. "But they couldn't figure it out. There didn't seem to be anything wrong with the door. She was really scared. She lives alone and thought that she might never get out."

Taken on its own merit and considered in a vacuum, it is easy to debunk everything that Julie's mom had to say about her time in the Chapel Street house as nothing more than circumstances of unusual but explainable actions. It's just as easy to lay blame at the clawed feet of her cats and identify them as the culprit for knocking items about and leaving them later to be found on the floor.

The little boy staring in her face as she awoke could have been nothing more than the end-piece of a dream.

*The soldier marching?*

Could be the pipes making noise or sounds otherwise coming from someone's television set above or below her apartment.

*Catching movement from the corner of her eye?*

She has cats.

*Her female cat won't lay on the bed anymore?*

Arthritis.

*The ghost cat seen running through her apartment?*

We have already established the fact that she has cats. Real cats. Maybe she is just confused about what she saw, because of her age. Maybe she heard Linda mention the story about

Bear's mom and that influenced her into believing that she saw the ghost cat as well. After all, she does have real cats in the apartment. Does she really know what she saw?

*The cats appear to be staring at something?*

What cat doesn't do that? That would be my question.

*Getting stuck in the shower?*

She's an old woman. The moisture and the steam caused the door to swell and it got stuck. And that is why the landlord couldn't find anything wrong with it later, after it had dried out.

If you wanted to debunk the suggestion of a haunting taking place at the Chapel Street residence then yes, you could quite easily come up with a reasonable explanation for everything that Julie's mom had to say about her experiences living in that particular location. The problem of course is that you can't just take what she had to say, view it in a vacuum and call that a fair assessment on what is allegedly happening there, because her story is just one version of a larger body of evidence that points to the fact that something supernatural is indeed going on. Her testimonial to the events that she has personally witnessed and spoken to is just one of three separate personal experiences that all follow the same general pattern and draw upon the same general conclusion. Is it reasonable to believe that everyone who either lives or lived in that house got it wrong or is otherwise making it up? Every single time? And if you want to go down that road, then what about West Street? At what point does it start to make more sense to simply acknowledge that something strange and otherworldly really is happening here?

C hapter 11: Boys in the Attic

Meanwhile, less than nine miles away LJ was getting a taste of his own supernatural experience. A former offensive lineman for a semi-professional New England football team, Larry junior was a mountain of a man. Not that size counts in matters where the supernatural is concerned. You know those hosts of popular ghost hunting shows, who puff their chest out and threaten the ghosts to either show themselves or else? That is not real life. That is an example of someone who has actually never seen a real ghost, and doesn't expect to see a real ghost. That is entertainment. That's akin to comparing professional wrestling to professional ice hockey. One is a real sport, and the other is scripted sports entertainment. In other words, it's fake! In real life, ghostly encounters are some combination of unsettling, frightening or even terrifying. Sometimes they are even violent (refer back to Richard's angry entity encounter or having his daughter getting her back scratched bloody for moving things around in the attic).

"There is a two-family house sitting just past the church (Saint John's Episcopal Parish Hill Church-the same church where my mom got married back in 1955!), that attic is full of activity," he told me.

It was a darkened autumn afternoon when LJ and his girlfriend had gone to watch a Patriots game with friends who were then living in the second floor apartment of the house on Hope Street, sitting smack dab between West Street and the demon house on Chesley Street, but on the other side of Central Street, which cut a path directly through the center of town.

"You could hear footsteps all day long, coming from the attic. Like someone was up there pacing. I wanted to go check it out, but my friends were dismissive about it. They didn't want to go up there," said LJ.

"Did they know that the place was haunted?" I asked.

"Yeah, they did. But they didn't mention it," he said. "So, eventually I got them to agree to go. The door to the attic was in the kitchen, and there was a bunch of stuff blocking it. We moved it all out of the way and I went first. The attic was pretty much down to the studs. The owner was planning on turning it into a third floor apartment. There was a box of old Christmas toys, like from the seventies up there, and as soon as I walked into the room Jingle Bells started playing. It was coming from an old Santa. We walked over to it in order to check it out. My friend was the one who picked it up, and when he turned it over we could see that it didn't have any batteries in it. As soon as he did that, the window opened by itself, then it slammed shut. After that, we all started to get a little frightened. Everyone went back downstairs."

It was all very interesting, and not dissimilar to what had been occurring on West Street since at least the 1950's. But LJ wasn't finished telling the story.

"After a little time had passed, three of us decided to go back up to the attic. There was kind of like a partial bathroom up there and above that was a crawl space. My buddy John works out all the time, so he started doing pull-ups off the end of the opening. He looked down to the end of it and he could see that there was nothing up there. Then, as he's hanging there, he feels a breath blow across the back of his neck, accompanied by a low growl."

"GET ME OUT OF HERE!!!" the friend shouted.

"Somehow he'd gotten hooked on a nail," recounted LJ. "So we ran over and helped him down."

At the same time that this was happening, LJ himself began to be overtaken by a strange feeling.

"I had the feeling that I was underwater," he told me. "I just felt off. We went back downstairs and I was just sitting on the couch rolling my fingers. You know? Like old people do.

My girlfriend had to drive us home. The next day, we drove to the grocery store. My girlfriend had to drive because I was still feeling off. As we entered the parking lot, I started to feel better. So I told her to head inside while I parked the truck. After that, I'm walking into the store and this eighty year old woman comes walking towards me, pushing her groceries. And she stops and looks at me. *I know who you are,* she said to me. *And I've been waiting for you."*

I've got to admit that when I first heard this story recounted to me it gave me chills. Sure, it could have just been the mindless musings of a senile old lady. But given the circumstances of the previous evening, taken in combination with the strange feeling that LJ had left the house on Hope Street with, and the possibility of a possession of some sort, it seemed at least possible that the creepy encounter with the old woman may have been something more than just coincidence.

Taken as a whole, it was an intense way to find out that your friend's house is haunted. But now he knew. What LJ didn't know was that one of his friends (the same one who had exposed the battery-less Santa) had been having vivid dreams about Quakers before that all happened, including a boy who kept trying to deliver an ominous and ambiguous warning. Quakers are members of a Protestant Christian sect that was highly persecuted in England and in North America in the seventeenth and eighteenth centuries. Members referred to each other as *friends* and met in meeting houses, such as the Friends Meeting House in nearby Uxbridge. One of the few places where Quakers could live and worship in relative peace was Rhode Island, including nearby settlements in Massachusetts, encompassing towns such as Millville, Uxbridge and the like. Their influence and presence in that particular area had indeed once been prominent. *But who dreams about Quakers, ever?* My bet is practically no one.

Built in 1900, "the house had a history," LJ told me. "The owner rents the house out now, but he used to live on the first floor. His wife died in that house. Now he lives down the street," he added. "Before my friends lived there, he had a family renting the upstairs apartment. They fought all the time, so he had to kick them out. There was also a handicapped boy who fell from a second floor window and died on the steps below. "

That owner that LJ mentioned is a man named William, and Norma is his second wife. Soon after he purchased the house in 2011 she told me that things began happening. Starting with an unsettling encounter in the basement.

"When my husband and his first wife initially purchased the house, his nephew was in the basement moving bricks for his father, who was doing some work on the house. He swore that he felt someone tap him on the shoulder. When he turned around he saw a man dressed in grey overalls who said, *'I'm not done with those yet.'* The nephew told the man that his dad was doing construction there and had told him to move the bricks, which he went back to doing. When he turned around again, the man was gone. There were no vehicles on the property to explain why someone else might have been down there. It just totally freaked him out. He left the basement after that and waited outside for his father to return. When he got back, the nephew refused to go back inside the house."

Later on, when a family friend agreed to come over in order to take a look at the electrical wiring in the attic, he reported to the couple that he'd seen orbs moving about the open space. On a separate occasion, another family friend became flustered when a curtain that she was trying to hang repeatedly fell from the window for no apparent reason. And although he did not recount this story to me personally, LJ told William that he'd seen the disarticulated head of a baby floating in the attic, while attempting to document the haunting with a video recorder.

Just like my grandmother's house on West Street, the house on Hope Street, where LJ had witnessed all these events, had also seen its share of death. But that didn't explain all of the hauntings sitting between West Street and the Conjuring House that were suddenly coming onto my radar. People die in houses all the time, and those houses don't go on to become haunted.

As far as I was concerned, there was something about the geography that was facilitating portal formation in this very specific stretch of land encompassing parts of south-central Massachusetts and extending down into the adjoining part of Rhode Island. The occurrence of hauntings clustered so close together seemed to defy the odds of statistical probability.

"The pub down on Main Street is also haunted, " said LJ.

Located on land that housed a former train station at the turn of the twentieth-century, and also a bowling alley, the pub he was referring to is today a popular local gathering place that is down the hill, across the Blackstone River and around the corner from both West Street and Hope Street, sitting just half a mile away from those two haunted locations, three if you want to count the "demon house" over on Chesley Street.

**The Millville train station circa the 1890's. Patrons of the modern-day pub that currently sits nearby report hearing the sounds of a ghost train as it pulls into the station that no longer exists. Photo courtesy of L. Clement.**

"My friend (the same one who rents the second floor apartment on Hope Street and exposed Santa) opens and closes the bar," LJ told me. "I've been there with him after closing. Sometimes you can hear the sounds of people bowling, and strikes."

I then asked if I could interview the friend.

"Nah, man. He won't talk to you about it," LJ informed me.

And hence is the reason why I haven't been using their names as I recounted LJ's experiences on Hope Street, but have instead merely been referring to them as 'friends.' Not everyone is comfortable attaching their name to or talking about phenomena that many or even most people have never experienced. What I have found over the years is that when you tell someone about a ghostly encounter that you've had, you invariably get hit with one of three typical reactions: *I don't think that you're lying but you probably misinterpreted what you saw.* Or: *You aren't remembering it correctly.* Or worst of all: *You were too young to know what you really saw.*

I've been guilty of it myself. Recently, as I was unloading my frustrations upon my daughter about not being able to get people to talk to me about their experiences for this book, she told me that she had seen two orbs from the bathroom mirror, hovering over my bed as she was leaning over the sink, brushing her teeth.

"I slammed the bathroom door shut," she told me. "It freaked me out."

Even though I know better, having had encounters with the supernatural in the past, I immediately discounted what she said. Why? Because *she's too young to actually know what an orb is or what it looks like.* That was my first thought. But I was already pre-biased on the subject because I'm absolutely certain that our house isn't haunted. At least, I don't think that it is. Haunted houses have a feeling to them, and I've never experienced it in that house. I could be wrong, though. It isn't out of the realm of possibility.

"It was probably just the reflection of headlights coming from one or two of the roads that bisect the property," I said.

"I know it wasn't headlights," she answered. But even now, I'm not convinced. And this is the problem that people have whenever they tell someone that they've seen something. I know it firsthand.

When I was a kid growing up in Florida, in a house sitting alongside a canal that emptied into the Gulf of Mexico, I looked in the water one afternoon and saw an octopus slowly floating up from the bottom of the canal, with all eight arms stretched out like a starfish. I was so excited! I had never seen one before, I couldn't wait to tell people what I saw. But when I did, no one believed me. *You didn't see an octopus,* I was told repeatedly. *It was probably a jellyfish.* I didn't get that, at all. It was so irritating to be dismissed like that. Like I didn't know the difference between an octopus and a jellyfish. It was all so stupid. I mean, they look nothing alike. It took some doing but I finally snapped a picture of it and proved conclusively that I was indeed seeing an octopus.

Frustrating but true. And that is why I think that lots of people who see ghosts don't want to talk about it. I eventually proved my story, courtesy of a Kodak camera and a roll of 110 film. But you can't just snap a picture of a ghost even if it's standing right in front of you. It most likely won't come out, and you won't prove anything for the effort. Even if you do capture something enticing, people are bound to say that it was photoshopped or that it is otherwise a fake, or at least explainable. All that you have is your word ultimately, and the other person's willingness to believe it.

Circling back to the local pub, the impressions made by its former incarnation as a bowling alley seemed to have made a lasting influence on the place, providing yet another example of sights and sounds from a past event being captured and ingrained on the fabric of time, subject to being replayed by the same catalyst or set of influences that allow hauntings and time slips to also take place. I started out looking to tell a story about one haunted house on West Street, and now I was up to nine different locations. There's no way that it was all just a coincidence.

# Chapter 12: The Hope Street Blues

I tried, man. I really did. On three different occasions, to be precise. But you can't make people talk about a subject if they don't want to discuss it with you. It's too bad too. I got really excited when LJ told me he had connections to other hauntings in town.

"I have another friend named Tim, who also lives on Hope Street," he told me. "His place is haunted too. He's seen decapitated ghosts in his living room."

"Do you think that Tim will give me an interview?" I asked.

"Yeah. He'll talk to you," said LJ. "I'll give him your information so that he can contact you."

"Great. Thanks," I replied.

"I think that I can get you into the attic where we encountered the ghosts too," he said. "The owner is a friend of mine. He said that any time that I wanted to come back to investigate it, he'd be thrilled. He knows that there are all kinds of activities taking place in that house."

That? I wasn't so sure of. I was already aware from talking to other people that spirits could attach themselves to you. And I sure as hell didn't want to bring anything home with me. I knew from talking to Richard and Brenda that something had followed them to their new address when they moved from West Street. LJ had left his first encounter on Hope Street feeling like a spirit had gotten inside of him. Amie Simard, the retired paranormal investigator that I interviewed for this book, told me that she had gotten out of the business after having kids specifically because she didn't want to bring anything home with her that might threaten her children. Ultimately though, it was too good of an offer to pass up.

"You know what? Let's do it," I replied. "Let me just check my schedule and figure out when I'm going to be available."

"I'll shoot him a message and let him know when you're available. I'm not gonna lie, I'd love another crack at that attic," said LJ, with a palpable excitement. "That was intense."

After several weeks of silence passed, I was beginning to feel like I'd been left at the altar. Again! Why was it that so few people wanted to talk to me about their experiences?

"Shoot. You didn't hear from them?" said LJ, when I reached out for the second time to try and figure out what was going on? "Something definitely had Tim spooked when I talked to him."

Maybe that was part of the problem. Maybe people just didn't want me stirring up the pot and making the situation worse for them.

"He wanted me to warn you to stay out of the woods in that area at night," continued LJ.

If that isn't an example of poking the bear, then I don't know what is. Naturally, I had to ask the obvious.

"What's going on in the woods at night?"

"There's lore about Lucy on the Lock," said LJ. "There are stories about a little girl who haunts the bike path. She can be both seen and heard."

The Lock is an historical landmark in town that serves as both a state park and an entry point to the Blackstone Greenway Bike Path. It is located on none other than the infamous Hope Street itself. Referred to as "New Village," the Hope Street neighborhood dates back to 1880 when it was developed as a series of two-family row houses for employees in Joseph Banigan's Woonsocket Rubber Company. In 1892, Banigan consolidated his company with eight other rubber manufacturers to form the U.S. Rubber Company, now known as Uniroyal, sitting as its first president before selling his stake for $9 million dollars. The neighborhood that he built for his employees was originally known as "Banigan's City." Banigan, who had arrived in Rhode Island in 1847 on the heels of the first wave of immigrants fleeing Ireland's great potato famine, was New England's first Irish-Catholic millionaire. Hope Street is one small part of his legacy to that town. Up until 1980, 98% of the town's population was of Irish-Catholic descent, many of whom like Banigan, had fled the potato famine, drawn to the Blackstone region for the numerous mill industries that promised gainful employment. This included my maternal grandfather Owen Mcgloin's family, as well as my paternal line. Smyth with a "Y" is the Irish spelling of the common last name that is usually spelled with an "I." My paternal grandfather, a man named Harold Smyth, was also a successful businessman of Irish descent, sitting as president of Stanley Woolen Mills for many years, owning one of the largest estates in the area (which just happened to be a stone's throw from Banigan City), or more commonly known now as Hope Street.

"I'll stay out of the woods at night," I told LJ. I had no problem doing that, but what else was going on I wondered?

"There's a ghost train that can be heard pulling into the old train station at night," I was told, an establishment currently operating as a popular Main Street pub. "There's also the ghost of an old lady down on Main Street who can be seen rocking on the porch. My friend Mark, his family owns the big house by the pub, that's haunted too. I used to go camping with them and they would tell me stories about the place."

"Will your friend Mark talk to me?" I asked.

"I'll send him a message," said LJ. But I never heard back.

As far as the train was concerned, Millville once had big plans for the railroad, undertaking the construction of three different lines at the same time, the Providence & Worcester railroad, the Boston & Hartford line and the Grand Trunk, that ambition coalescing into the construction of the Triad Bridge. As originally planned out in the 1800's, these spans would have allowed boat traffic to pass along the Blackstone canal unencumbered while all three railroads crisscrossed the area at the same time.

This is the exact spot where all three rail lines would have crossed each other. The paving stones sit atop the old Boston & Hartford bed, the currently active Providence & Worcester line runs directly below. In the background is one of two concrete abutments for the Grand Trunk.

As it turned out, the Grand Trunk rail line (which ran above and parallel to both the Boston & Hartford railway and West Street) was never finished. The Boston & Hartford line was pulled up in 1955, its bed being the foundation for the bike path currently sitting at that location. Only the Providence & Worcester Railway remains, its trains passing through the area on a nightly basis. Is this the true source of the sound that people are mistaking for the "ghost train," as it pulls into the station that's no longer there? I don't know. But the question needs to be asked.

**One of the abutments for the never-finished Grand Trunk rail line indicates the direction in which the train would have crossed the Triad Bridge in Millville, had it ever been completed. In the center of the top portion is the partial date 19–, with the decade having crumbled away.**

Going back to the Lucy on the Lock story, it's interesting in that it's similar to another story I read in Worcester Magazine about another Lucy in another town. According to the legend, five year old Lucy Keyes followed her two older sisters into the woods of Sterling on the morning of April 14, 1755, as they traveled down to the banks of Wachusett Lake to collect sand for their mother. Trailing behind her older siblings, Lucy lost the trail and was never seen again. No one ever found out what happened to the unfortunate girl, but her father was said to be having a property dispute with a neighbor by the name of Tilly Littlejohn, who supposedly confessed to killing the girl on his deathbed and hiding her body in a hollowed out log. An Indian abduction was also considered, bolstered by the discovery of a white woman living with a tribe near the Canadian border. Although she knew very little English, she did indicate that she once lived near "Chusett Hill," a suspiciously close iteration of Mount Wachusett. Whatever happened to the unfortunate young girl, legend has it that her mother spent years after the disappearance searching the nearby woods and calling out her name. It was long said that the ghost of little Lucy could still be both seen and heard haunting the woods of the Sterling countryside. Was this the same Lucy making an appearance at the Millville Lock, some 40 miles away?

Maybe not.

As I tried to dig deeper into the background of the Lucy on the Lock story, I uncovered a similar story about a "Lucy on the Lock" in Millville, Ohio. It was beginning to feel like one too many Lucy stories for comfort. More like a recycled urban legend than a real story. Then I learned of yet another little ghost girl in the woods story. This time down in Burrillville. Home to the

Conjuring House.

Croft Road leads to the Buck Hill Scout Reservation, down in Pascoag, Rhode Island. Pascoag itself is one of the eight villages that comprise the larger community known as Burrillville.

"Over where the Boy Scout camp is, near Jackson Schoolhouse Road, there's a place where people go off-roading and there're power-line trails and stuff. Well, by the Boy Scout camp over there, there's a sharp corner down by the campground, where people dump random piles of junk, lots of people say that if you drive down there at night that you can see a girl, and it's supposed to be the ghost of a girl who got hit by a car," explained one longtime resident who grew up on Round Top Road, but had since moved away.

"How did a little girl get hit by a car on a dirt road where people go off-roading?" I asked.

"The Boy Scout Camp goes over there," she said.

So now I had four little ghost girl stories. But at least this one wasn't named Lucy (as far as I could discern). Closer to home, I couldn't say if there was a ghost named Lucy haunting the Millville Lock or not, but there was an historical catalyst for just such a haunting.

The Central Street train station once stood on the site of the modern-day parking lot for the current bike path at Millville Lock. On an evening in the early part of the 1950's, tragedy struck when a family by the name of Dumas were caught stopped on the tracks of the Boston & Hartford railway, where a locomotive plowed into the family's stalled vehicle, destroying it in the process and scattering debris and body parts like so much dust to the wind. It's reasonable to assume that this tragedy resulted in at least one member of the doomed family sticking around after the fact. Sudden, violent and unexpected deaths are thought to be one cause for hauntings being linked to a specific location, and this would explain it. Was Lucy really the ghost of the Dumas girl killed in the accident? Maybe I couldn't get into the attic on Hope Street, but I could pay a visit to the supposedly haunted Lock.

The exact spot where the Dumas family met their untimely demise in the first half of the 1950's. Their car was stopped on the tracks of the Boston & Hartford railroad when a train passed through and hit the vehicle broadside. Did this tragedy give rise to the Lucy on the Lock haunting? Photo courtesy of L. Clement.

The Central Street train station was located on the site of the current parking lot for the Lock and bike path. It was smaller than the station on Main Street. Photo courtesy of L. Clement.

# CHAPTER 13: LOCK AND KEYES

The Millville Lock, with its report of a ghost girl named Lucy haunting the surrounding woods runs parallel with Hope Street, where hauntings at two different addresses have been reported. West Street starts at the building on the left.

I'm not going to lie about it or dress up the truth for the sake of telling a good story. I didn't expect to see or hear any ghosts when my daughter and I visited the Millville Lock and bike path, on a warm and sunny afternoon back on the fourteenth of August, in the late summer of 2024. First of all, it wasn't nighttime, and I'd been warned to stay out of the woods specifically at night by one Hope Street resident, who otherwise declined to give me an interview. The problem that I had as a visitor is that unless you live nearby and can access the path through your backyard, it isn't really feasible to investigate the Lock at night. The park closes at dusk and is patrolled by local police looking for vandals, vagrants, teens hanging out and drinking booze, not to mention trespassers of one stripe or another (which I'm sure includes people looking for ghosts). It's not like you can just drive up in the dark and take a look around without being caught and sent on your way. It's probably possible, but it wasn't worth the hassle to me. And besides that, I wasn't jumping up and down for an opportunity to go into the woods at night. That can go sideways in more ways than one, the least of which would be encountering a ghost.

Secondly, experiencing the supernatural is a crapshoot. It's not like you can plan on it just because something has happened at a particular spot in the past. Even at my grandmother's place, I only experienced something strange on a couple of occasions, while other people said it happened all the time. So I wasn't surprised or disappointed by that outcome. I wasn't expecting to see anything otherworldly, and we didn't. Plus, hauntings have a feeling. And I wasn't picking up that vibe. What I hoped to accomplish was to get a better understanding of the lay of the land, and use that knowledge to see if I could come up with an alternate explanation for some of the stories that I was hearing. I mean, it's one thing to say that something is haunted, and it's another to be left without any other rational conclusion after considering all of the contributing factors.

Millville itself is actually the second youngest town in the state of Massachusetts, having been incorporated barely 100 years ago, in 1916. It was originally part of the town of Blackstone, which was originally part of nearby Mendon. The entire region was first settled by Europeans in 1662 and was originally inhabited by the Nipmuc tribe. The key catalyst for all of this settlement was the Blackstone River, whose flowing waters were an integral factor in providing food and fresh water to early settlers, as well as a mode of transportation and a way to link commerce in the years before the railroads were built, during a time when public roads were rough and passage unreliable.

The initiative for building a canal came from merchants in Providence, Rhode Island, who wished for an efficient and reliable means for the transportation of goods which would allow them to profit from trading with the farming communities of the Blackstone Valley and the merchants of Worcester. The Blackstone Canal Company was formed in 1823 after being successfully delayed for several years by commercial interests in Boston, who didn't want to lose their influence on overland trade with central Massachusetts. Construction began in 1825, at a cost of $750,000 (twice as much as it was budgeted for) and was dug out by hand, primarily by the same Irish-American immigrants that had been responsible for building the Erie Canal. It was engineered by Benjamin Wright and Holmes Hutchinson. Wright had been chief engineer on the Erie Canal project, while Hutchinson had cut his teeth working on the canals of New York.

Construction on the canal itself, the lock and the towpath, as it pertained to Millville, began in the fall of 1827 and then continued after the spring thaw of 1828. The overall project was completed that same year, in October of 1828, when a packet named *Lady Carrington* became the first vessel to complete the two day trip from Providence to Worcester. The finished product was thirty-five feet wide and ran for forty-five miles, during which it intersected the Blackstone River sixteen times. Because it ascended 451 feet from Providence to Worcester, a series of forty-nine locks were designed to facilitate canal traffic by controlling the level of water that a vessel needed to pass through. Each lock was made of granite blocks resting on a wooden foundation. They were seventy-feet long and ten feet wide, housing a thick wooden gate at each end, held in place by iron pinions.

**The best preserved lock still in existence is lock #21 in Millville. Each lock was 70 feet long, ten feet wide with an average water depth of 4-4.5 feet deep. The average lift for each lock was just over 9 feet.**

A towpath could be found on either side of the canal and was attended by two horses of no particular breed. These horses would pull each boat along the canal a total distance of fifteen miles a day, before working in the opposite direction the following day. It was, in its day, state of the art technology, enriching merchants from Worcester to Providence and throughout the Blackstone Valley, providing a spark to the Industrial Revolution that followed and serving as a catalyst for numerous mills and factories to open throughout the area.

But Boston interests had not given up on controlling the flow of commerce, opening a rail line to Worcester in 1835. That same year, rail lines were established between Lowell and Boston and Boston and Providence. But it was the opening of the Providence & Worcester Railroad in 1847 that served as the death knell for the Blackstone Canal Company, with the canal ceasing operations only one year later. As the newest available technology at the time, the canal couldn't compete with the rails speed and efficiency. For investors of the Blackstone Canal Project, it was a major financial blow and ultimately a commercial failure for its investors, operating for a total of only twenty years.

**The Providence & Worcester Railroad, which ran parallel to the Blackstone Canal, killed off its rival one year after it was opened in 1847. The rail line is still in use today.**

One of the things that I wanted to look at when I visited the Millville Lock was the layout of the railroad in consideration to its proximity to Main Street and the pub where ghostly activity had been reported. I'd been told that in its previous incarnations that the property surrounding the area had housed a bowling alley and a train station. Patrons of that establishment had at different times reported hearing the sounds of bowling taking place, but also the sounds of a train as if it were pulling into a station. I'm not certain when the old train station was torn down, but the Boston & Hartford rail line ceased operations in 1955, possibly making the need for a train station expendable in that area. Even though the Providence & Worcester rail line continues to pass through town to this day. Today, the Millville Public Library occupies that very same spot on Main Street. As for the Bowling alley, it had its place on Main in the years leading up to World War I, before becoming The Town Cafe, and then Duffy's Tavern, before finally ending up as the establishment that the Thirsty Thursday crowd knows it as today.

## Bowling in Millville

This week's Attic Treasure comes from George Seagrave of Pascoag, who received a copy of this picture when he ran the Town Cafe (now Duffy's Tavern) on Main Street

Dean, Mike Hession, and Gene Flynn in front of th Millville Bowling Alley in the center of that town. M Seagrave believes the photo dates from before Wor War I.

**The Millville Bowling Alley entertained the local populace down on Main Street in the early decades of the twentieth-century. It also served as a pool hall. Today, a popular Main Street pub occupies the land where the bowling alley once sat.**

Patrons of the pub report hearing strikes in the after-hours, as well as the sound of people bowling, a hundred years after the lanes themselves closed down. Photo courtesy of L. Clement.

This four story building on Main Street once housed the bowling alley and pool hall. After a fire destroyed most of the building, only the first floor was salvaged. Today it operates as a popular drinking establishment. Photo courtesy of L. Clement.

Whatever the truth is, the fact is that the modern Providence & Worcester Railway passes through town twice a day. Not very far from the pub itself. Is this what people are hearing as the "ghost train" pulls into the station that long ago ceased to exist? Or is the sound of an old Boston & Hartford locomotive that used to stop in the area embedded onto the fabric of time, in much the same way that Roman soldiers keep marching across the basement of the Treasurer's House in England?

**Once upon a time, this bike path was the rail bed for the old Boston & Hartford Railroad. The tracks were removed in 1955. Does a ghost train still pass through here on its way to Boston?**

I don't know what the answer is, having never experienced the phenomenon myself. I only know what other people have said.

But given the extent of paranormal activity that is reported to be taking place in the surrounding area, I definitely would not discount the possibility of a ghost train stopping in at the current pub. The one caveat to the theory that the current railroad is causing the sounds attributed to the ghost train is that the modern Providence & Hartford railway does not stop in Millville, and thus would not be making the distinct sound of a train as it pulls into a station.

As far as the little ghost girl named Lucy is concerned, I feel the same way about her that I feel about the ghost train. I don't know if there is any substance to the story or not, but as I walked the bike path I did notice that the only thing separating it from the Hope Street neighborhood on the left was a thin strand of woods, no more than twenty-feet in length, with backyards pushing right up against the foliage separating the two. Many of those properties had dirt paths cutting directly over to the bike path.

**A home can be seen through the woods from the bike path at the Millville Lock, the backyard of which pushes up against the brush line.**

The proximity of these homes made me wonder if the sounds of real children playing in their own backyards was being mistaken at times by superstitious minds for something more otherworldly than what it really is. It would be super easy for neighborhood kids to access the bike path and then "disappear" again. The problem is that even though I haven't seen Lucy for myself, the fact that there are dozens of hauntings taking place in that specific area (two of which I've seen for myself), makes me wonder if there isn't some truth to the story. I certainly did not hear or see anything that would confirm or debunk what I'd been told based on my one visit. But that doesn't mean that it isn't so. At the end of the day, all that I really proved was that there were some potentially built-in explanations for the phenomena that had been reported. As with most things ghost related, in cases in which you have not had the privilege to see it for yourself, you're stuck with the burden of weighing the evidence against the likelihood of a claim, consider the source and draw your conclusion.

The path that the Grand Trunk Railroad would have taken as it passed through Millville on its way to the Triad Bridge above the Blackstone River.

The original path of the Boston & Hartford Railroad as it runs parallel to West Street. My grandmother's house had a wide, dirt path that opened directly onto the old bed, and then continued across and through a tangle of woods, over an old foot bridge straddling a culvert, to an open field on the other side that climbed a steep hill leading to the bed of the never-completed Grand Trunk.

Four concrete footings can be seen rising from the waters of the Blackstone River. These would have supported the train trestle of the Grand Trunk as it crossed the river and turned left for a rendezvous with the Boston & Hartford and the Providence & Worcester Railroads at the Triad Bridge.

C hapter 14: Over a Barrel on Ironstone Street

Long before patrons of the pub down on Main Street reported hearing echoes of its distant past, there was another former bar and flop house around the corner and up on Ironstone Street that seemed to be trying to recapture some former glory of its own, in much the same way that customers and employees of the popular modern-day establishment could still hear the ghost train stopping in at the once upon a time train station, or the sound of people bowling on lanes that had not existed in decades.

The house in question had originally been built in 1889 as a watering hole for the hard-working residents of Banigan's City, who could drop in for a drink or two after a hard day's toil laboring in the mills set up along the Blackstone River, and then sleep it off in the "hotel" that comprised the other half of the building, should it become necessary. It was also a not-too-distant walk for passengers disembarking from either of the two train stations in town, one on nearby Main Street and the other on Central. Jane came to the property by marriage, and by the time that her husband's grandparents got their hands on it, the house's better days seemed to be already behind it.

"It was somewhat run down when the family bought it," she said, referring to the home that had since been converted to a duplex. "But they got to work on fixing it up. There were some weird things happening there."

Soon after moving in, it was the grandmother of Jane's husband who first began to hear the sound of barrels, as if they were being rolled across the basement floor. The only problem was, there were no barrels in the basement! A deeper investigation into the sound revealed that the house had a secret sub-basement that had previously been sealed off. Mystery solved?

Well, not exactly.

It was inferred by the family that the barrels of liquor dated back to the late nineteenth to early twentieth-century, and the house's stint as a bar. In an age without electronic refrigeration, the sub-basement with its dirt floor would have provided a cool and dark environment that would have extended the shelf life of the booze and prevented it from spoiling. It made total sense. But that ultimately did not explain the noise that the house was making.

To begin with, nobody knew that the second basement was even there. So how was it that the barrels were moving in the first place? Nobody was down there to move them. Secondly, the sub-basement had a dirt floor, and this did not match the mechanics of the sound that was being heard in the living space above, since barrels rolling over a dirt floor barely make any noise of consequence. It didn't mesh with what the family said they were hearing, and the sound did not match up with the reality of where the barrels were actually sitting. Just like my experience on West Street (one street over from Ironstone), where I had pulled the bedroom curtain aside to expose the broken window pane, after seeing the curtain strangely blow to the ceiling in the middle of winter, the broken glass seemed to explain what I had seen, but it didn't account for the storm window being closed behind it, or the fact that it wasn't blowing outside. Much like the San Francisco cityscape of 1906, that explanation was sitting on shaky ground. It really wanted to be the reason for the witnessed phenomenon. But in the final analysis, it just didn't add up.

It's doubtful that the barrels stored in the sub-basement had anything to do with the sounds that were being heard. How could they have? It seems more plausible that in the house's past history as a bar room, that the sound of barrels being rolled down to the sub-basement for storage was a common feature of the daily operations of the business that existed there, and that this distinct sound had been captured and ingrained in the fabric of time, just like the bowling and train station sounds still being heard at the bottom of the hill, down on Main Street. In any event, if the sound of rolling barrels was the only thing going on in the house on Ironstone Street, then that would have been creepy enough. But unfortunately, it wasn't.

Jane moved out of the tenant apartment of the duplex after her father-in-law passed away in the house in 1975. After she left, her sister-in-law Diane moved into the vacant apartment. Diane never heard the barrels rolling about, but she was frequently perplexed by the sound of someone climbing the stairs when no one was actually using them. At the time, her pregnant daughter was staying with her. One afternoon as the daughter was taking a nap, she awoke to the sensation of someone touching her stomach. At first it was confusing, since she was alone in the bedroom. But then she looked down to see the impression of a handprint stretched across her pregnant belly.

"I believe he was there protecting her and her unborn child," said Michelle, of her father, the man who had been the owner of the house, and had recently passed away.

It was also true that Diane's daughter's two dogs were fixated on one particular spot in the house. It just happened to be the exact location where Michelle's dad died.

Then one day in 1977, while Diane was wrapping presents in the kitchen, she heard the Christmas bells that she had strung up in the living room begin to ring loudly.

"When I went into the living room, the bells were ringing violently. There was no logical reason for it. I told the landlady and she said that she would have the house blessed," she said.

As I was preparing to wrap this chapter up and call it finished, I got a message from a woman named Ellen, who told me that she had babysat for a woman named Michelle back in the 1970's, and that her house on Ironstone had been "super haunted."

It didn't take much effort to figure out that she was referring to the same house that I had already written about.

"I used to babysit for a woman when I was a teenager, who lived in a house that had once been a saloon," she said.

*'A saloon?' I thought. How many saloons and bars had there been on Ironstone Street?*

"What was her name?" I asked.

"Michelle."

*Ding ding ding ding ding ding ding* went the alarm bells in my head. We have a match! It's always an exciting moment for me when I get corroborating information from disparate individuals who have either never met, or haven't seen each other in fifty years.

"Tell me what you saw."

"When I was babysitting I would hear the sound of barrels rolling around downstairs," recalled Ellen. "The lights would flicker and the power would go out. Doors would open by themselves and I would hear the sound of people talking, like saloon talk. I know this sounds crazy, but the barrels would be rolling around downstairs and then the door to the cellar would open. It would suddenly get very, very cold. And you could hear the sound of a bunch of glasses clinking together. Sometimes I would fall asleep on the couch, and I would get woken up by a draft coming through the living room and the sound of clinking glasses. It got to the point where I wouldn't babysit there anymore unless my boyfriend agreed to come with me."

For Ellen, that was all that she had to say about her time spent in that particular house, although she did have more to say about the street itself. As for this address, another death would occur on the property in 2000, when Jane's first husband suffered a heart attack while doing yard work and died on the lawn.

Jane's mother-in-law went into a nursing home in the 1990's and sold the property to Jane's sister and her husband, who still own the old saloon to this day.

C hapter 15: The Burning Question

Like I said, I was excited when I heard from Ellen. That conversation provided me with additional details regarding the house on Ironstone Street that I had not previously been privy to. But it was what she said next that I found especially interesting. Ellen had grown up on Ironstone Street, and as a young girl she had watched a young man commit suicide right in the driveway next to where she and a friend had been playing. His mother would commit suicide in that same house just two years later and father twenty years after that. Not only that, but the man who bought the property later on also killed himself in that very same house. Was it all just a strange and tragic coincidence or was there something more nefarious than that going on?

This is not necessarily a story about a haunting, but I wanted to include it because there was obviously some seriously bad *juju* going down on Ironstone Street back in the '70's. And given the extent of the paranormal activity taking place all around that area, it at least needs to be asked if there wasn't something more than just bad family dynamics at play here. Although I have already concluded in my own mind that the source of all of this paranormal activity is related to electromagnetic energy being given off by some related geographical catalyst, the question still gets asked if the land that Millville was built upon wasn't already cursed before the very first house was even erected. Was this indeed bloodstained soil dating all the way back to the pre-colonial era? Was the land sacred to the Native American cultures that existed here first, and did they bury their dead here?

Here's the thing. I don't believe in curses, but there are those who will ask these questions and then point to tragedies like the one that occurred on Ironstone Street as proof of its existence. Here's what Ellen told me about that terrifying afternoon:

"Tom Brophy owned a house on Ironstone Street that always creeped me out. When I was a little kid, maybe five or six, I was playing with a friend on the side of a driveway leading down to that house, and Tom's oldest son came running past us. He was in high school I think. A member of the track team. After he went by, he ran into his yard where he doused himself in gasoline and set himself on fire. Then he wandered out into the driveway where we were playing. I freaked out and ran home to get my dad. He ran back with a blanket and put the fire out, but the boy died anyway," Ellen recalled. "I will never forget him stumbling out into the driveway totally engulfed in flames. It was very traumatic."

Also traumatized by the events that transpired that day was the boy's mother, who proceeded to kill herself inside the home just a few years after it happened. Twenty years after the fact, Tom also killed himself with a gun, inside the family's home. But what's strange, is that the man who bought the house after that also shot himself to death, marking four exceptionally violent suicides all taking place in the same house or on the accompanying property.

"The guy who bought the house lived there for a few years," added Ellen. "One afternoon he stopped by to talk to my mom. He had a bunch of candy with him and he asked her if she wanted it, because he had noticed that she always had kids in the front yard. My mom declined the offer because she wasn't comfortable with taking candy from someone that she hardly knew. She said *no thank you* and closed the door on the guy. She felt bad after the fact because she found out that he had gone home and shot himself."

Planning to kill himself, he had probably made the offer as one final act of kindness. Maybe he had the candy in the house and figured that it shouldn't go to waste. Either way, his suicide made for death number four.

"I always had a bad feeling about that house," Ellen

concluded. "I don't know if it's a thing, or if there is actually something to it."

Chapter 16: The Kempton Road Mystery

Lee doesn't know why his house is haunted. But like so many other nearby properties in the town in which he lives, he's had experiences.

"It's strange, and I don't know why this would be," he said to me. "Because I built this place myself back in 1984, and I know that nothing bad has ever happened in this house, or anything like that. But weird things have occurred here."

It all started one night as Lee's wife lay sleeping on the living room couch, recovering from a medical procedure and unable to climb the stairs to the bedroom on the second floor.

"She was laid up for seven months," he recalled, "and I would sleep on the other couch so that I could be close by in case she needed something."

On the night in question, Lee awoke to find a woman that he'd never seen before sitting on his living room floor, staring him in the face.

"What are you doing here?" he asked the woman, who was wearing an old-time dress that was long and decorated with a flower pattern. "She had long brown hair that was hanging down past her shoulders, and was resting on the floor with her elbows sitting on top of her knees and her head in her hands."

Her countenance was one of nonchalant interest, as if she were engaged in watching a television program. When Lee turned to check on his wife, to make sure that she was still on the couch, he looked back again and she was gone.

"My wife didn't believe me," said Lee. "But I know that I was awake."

More convincing to the missus, was the morning that the couple were in the kitchen making breakfast.

"We were downstairs fixing breakfast and we heard the

sound of someone walking around on the second floor. We were home alone at the time, so we knew that nobody should have been up there."

Thinking that they had an intruder in the house, he grabbed a weapon and headed upstairs to investigate the unexplained footsteps filtering down through the kitchen ceiling.

*"I'm just letting you know,"* he called out in warning, as he climbed the stairs to the second floor, *"I have a gun."*

When he got to the top, Lee could find no evidence that anyone had been up on the home's second level. He could find no explanation for the footsteps that both he and his wife had heard from the kitchen. Nothing bad had ever happened in that house. Lee said so himself. There was no prior indication for a haunting to be taking place in the home. But he also knew that the same thing wasn't necessarily true about the surrounding neighborhood that he lived in. Let's talk about the Gagne mystery.

Mrs. Gagne was a woman of habit. She lived at the very end of the street during the 1950's, and for many years she was a familiar figure in this part of town, as neighbors would frequently see her walking down Kempton Road to the corner market down on Main Street, looking to buy goods and groceries for the family. Then she could be seen walking back home again. Until the day that she wasn't seen at all. It seemed as though she had just disappeared from the face of the earth, never to be seen again. When Mr. Gagne showed up at the market to buy his own groceries some time later, the butcher asked him where his wife was.

"She's gone," he replied, in a sharp and defensive tone. "And she ain't never coming back."

aphy

ɘ

(122)

Forest View Dr

Kempton Rd

Chestnut Hill Rd

Chestnut Hill Rd

Albee Rd

Chestnut Hill Rd

Blackstone River

Chestnut Hill Rd

Millville    Lincoln

**Kempton Road branches off Chestnut Hill Road, where three other hauntings have been reported. Each day, Mrs. Gagne could be seen walking down to Main Street (Route 122) and then back again, until the day that she disappeared. Courtesy of Google Maps.**

A police search of the neighborhood and the surrounding area, as well as an investigation into the woman's disappearance turned up nothing. No trace of Mrs. Gagne was ever found, and a re-evaluation of the case in the mid 1980's also turned up no clues. No one was ever charged with a crime related to the disappearance, and no one ever found out what happened to her. But that wasn't the only event of infamy that Kempton Road could lay claim to.

A full decade before she went missing under mysterious circumstances, the property that the Gagne's would later own had been the scene of another gruesome tragedy.

"There was a man who owned that property," Lee told me. "Back in the 1940's. He committed suicide by throwing himself on a saw. You know, the kind with a long chain attached to it. He was nearly decapitated. It happened in the barn. There used to be a big red barn on that property, but it's not there anymore."

After the incident with the unexplained footsteps over his kitchen ceiling, things settled down for Lee and his wife. But every now and then he thinks that he still sees something moving about the house.

"I always think that I see something out of the corner of my eye," he noted. And the reason may have something to do with a photo taken in his shed.

On one occasion when Lee was reviewing footage taken from a security system set up in his shed, he noted that the camera had taken a picture of a strange image floating near the top of the ceiling. It was cloudy in appearance, long, indistinct, wispy and not too dissimilar from what others had captured in trying to take pictures of ghosts that they were seeing. It puts to mind the wonder of what Mrs. Gagne might have been wearing on the day that she went missing. Could it have been a flowery dress? It's true that nothing bad ever happened inside the house that Lee built. But what secrets does the land upon which it sits hold?

This unexplained image was taken by a motion-sensitive security camera in a shed on Kempton Road. Wispy, indistinct foggy images are frequently captured via standard photography when trying to capture the image of a ghost. Photo courtesy of Lee C.

C hapter 17: Mayhem on Miller Street

Devin's brother is a brave man. He's tough, he's strong, and he's a member of the Marine Corps. He also won't stay in the house on Miller Street at night when he comes to visit his brother.

"He sleeps at his friend's house instead," Deven notes with amusement, in giving consideration to the stark contradiction between what he does for a living and where he chooses to sleep and why.

When Devin and his family moved to Millville in 1987, they undoubtedly thought they were moving into a nice, quiet suburban neighborhood in a quaint New England town, complete with friendly townsfolk and a good school system.

*Check, check and check.*

But what they probably didn't realize, nor could they possibly have predicted, was that they would also be taking up residence in one of the most haunted stretches of land in all of Massachusetts, if not the entirety of New England itself, with at least two dozen hauntings occurring all within a tiny one-mile radius from the Miller Street address that they were to eventually call home.

"You always get a weird feeling when you're in that house," Deven noted, "especially upstairs," he added, referring to the place where his family has lived for the past twenty-two years.

"In our house you see quick shadows," added older brother Dillon. "Nothing that is defined as a person or anything like that, just a quick, black shadow that makes you look to see who it is."

In consideration of most of the encounters detailed in this book, the Miller Street haunting is in a class by itself. Comparatively speaking, the majority of the ghosts, the phenomena and the experiences witnessed by those residents who were willing to share their stories with me, have for the most part all fallen into the same category of manifestation. In fact, it seems as though many of the details themselves could be swapped out one story for the other and nobody would know the difference. The ghosts themselves have generally been benign, their actions curious, their presence elusive and their stories interesting. But not at this Miller Street address. This haunting is flat out different. As I said to Deven himself when we communicated for the first time.

"By the way," I said, in wrapping up our discussion, "these are some of the scariest stories that anyone has told me yet."

And I meant it.

Let's start with something creepy, but less aggressive and frightening. They've got a mimic in the house. A mimic is a type of ghost (or demon) who uses the voice of a trusted family member to call out to a specific individual, in order to mess with or gain the trust of that person, for reasons that are unclear. Whether they are calling out to screw with someone's head or setting that person up to be taken advantage of in some way, these kinds of encounters are not good. At the very least, it is like being toyed with. At worst, it may be trying to draw the person in so that it can spring a trap of sorts, something more frightening where the entity may be feeding off the fear and heightened emotions of the target. It's possible that they just do it for amusement. But any way you slice it, this is bad news. It is as Deven himself told me:

"Sometimes I would hear my mom calling out to me, but she wouldn't even be home at the time."

Scarier still was the time she was home and asked Deven to go upstairs to retrieve something from her room.

"I went upstairs one night to grab something for my mom. Her bedroom door was open halfway, and as I approached it I noticed a hand slowly coming out from around the edge of the door. There wasn't supposed to be anyone in there. I didn't know if we had an intruder in the house or what, so I kicked the door open and turned on all of the lights. But nobody was in there."

Sometimes he would be sitting in his own bedroom, only to hear things being moved about in his closet. Big things. But when he looked, there would be nothing in there to explain all the noise that he'd been hearing.

Worse still was the times that he did know where the noise was coming from.

"At the top of the stairs is an old cast iron heating vent grate cover. At random, it would come loose and go flying down the hallway, go around the corner and smash into my bedroom door. If the dog was in the way, it would hit her."

Although he hasn't seen her for himself, others in the family have seen the ghost of a young girl going up and down the stairs. The family believes that it is the ghost of Sara Miller.

"The Miller's were the original owners of the house, going back to the early twentieth century. The house was built in 1900. The street itself is named after them. We knew that they were buried at the Millville Cemetery," Deven said, "so we went up there one day and found the family plot. Sure enough, there was a girl named Sara Miller, who died young and was buried with the family."

Central to the story of many of the hauntings that I covered has been the appearance of a little ghost girl. It has been a key element in numerous paranormal encounters that have been reported. Less common (thankfully) has been the appearance of the shadow people.

"One night, me and my buddy went out late to have a fire," Deven recalled. "But when we got to the backyard, he stopped and said *dude, look!* Inside the junk car that was parked in the yard were two red eyes looking back at us. We ran back a few feet, then turned around again. It was now outside the car, peeking around an old, empty chicken coop. We then ran inside to grab a flashlight, but when we got back it was gone. We never saw it again, but a few years later, my nephew saw the same thing in the same place. I later learned that when we were kids, my sisters would sometimes see red eyes looking in the window. I know that the red eye thing is hard to believe," Deven admitted. "But

THE WEST STREET HAUNTING

that's what we saw. I don't ever tell anyone about the red eyes because I always feel like people think that I'm lying. Which is understandable."

One person who wouldn't think he was lying was West Street Richard. He'd already seen something similar sitting on the roof of his own house just half a mile away from the Miller Street address.

Shadow people are another type of paranormal manifestation that falls outside the box of your typical, average, ordinary, run of the mill haunting. As rare as it is to see a ghost in the average person's lifetime, this counts as being much rarer than even that. They appear as dark shadow-like figures in human form that may be solid or foggy, child-sized or adult in appearance. They are sometimes seen to be wearing a hat, a hood or a cloak, but they may also have nothing on top of their head at all. Their eyes have been reported to glow red, green, white, or to be absent altogether. Of these, the red eye shadow people are thought to be the most malevolent, and confrontation with a red-eyed shadow person should be avoided at all costs. It is unclear exactly what they are, but theories abound.

One suggestion is that they are the spiritual remnants of humans who were evil in life, and that because they have not repented or accepted their current fate, that they are stuck in limbo, somewhere between this existence and the next, trying to avoid going to hell or paying the bill due on a lifetime of bad karma. They differ from ghosts in that they lack recognizable facial features and clothing, but rather manifest as dark silhouettes in human form, with profiles that can sometimes be seen to flicker in and out of a person's peripheral vision. Unlike ghosts, who appear to be either stuck in transition or trying to hold on to the past, shadow people are actively trying to avoid their fate by refusing to move into the next plane of existence. This subtle difference explains why ghosts appear much the same way as they did in life, while shadow people are expressed with an absence of light.

Although they can sometimes be seen in haunted places

concurrent with other phenomena, and may be mistaken as ghosts themselves, shadow people generally present, manifest and behave in ways that are different from other spiritual encounters. For one thing, sightings are most always accompanied by feelings of fear, dread and uneasiness. They are typically seen lurking about and when observed, are caught staring at those who see them. Some people suggest that these are not a form of ghost at all, but are entirely demonic in nature. Nearly everyone agrees that whatever it is that these manifestations might actually be, they are not good.

To hear Deven tell it, even with all of the things he told me, he has gotten off easier than his siblings have.

"There are so many other stories that my siblings could tell you," he said. "I have probably had the least amount of encounters out of all of us."

Maybe so. But can any of your siblings say that they've been photobombed by a ghost?

This enlarged image taken from a photo that was posted on a social media site, shows the translucent outline of a balding man passing behind the couple in the foreground. According to Devin, he was not seen or detected in real time and was only noticed by friends after the picture had already been posted.

C hapter 18: Orbs, Entities and Things Much Worse

True to his word, when Devin added me to a group chat including his mom and siblings, I soon began to get an avalanche of stories regarding the family home on Miller Street that set my mind to wondering. My first thought was that this particular haunting was so extensive, varied and different that it probably deserved to be a stand-alone book all in its own right. I rolled the notion over for a day or two, trying to piece together in my mind how I would approach a separate project like that. I liked the idea of getting two books out of this research, *The West Street Haunting* and *The Miller Street Haunting.* But the problem is this, none of these hauntings are stand-alone events. I'm convinced that they all have a related catalyst, and as such they all deserve to be told together. Because at the end of the day, it really is all about one giant ghost story.

The other thing that I thought about was that I had unintentionally uncovered a haunting that rivaled what was going on down in Harrisville, Rhode Island. Aside from the "Demon House" over on Chesley Street, which I was struggling to dig up much information on other than the fact that the family had been driven out of their house on two occasions, the Miller Street address really was Millville's own version of the famous Conjuring House in Burrillville.

According to Devin's mom, a woman named Rose, strange things began happening right after the family moved to Miller Street back in 1987.

"I was sitting on the floor in the back living room putting curtains onto curtain rods," she told me, "and I saw a round light about the size of a softball cross in front of me and slowly proceed to move across the room and out the open window. Even though it was a single ball of light and not characteristic of headlights passing through the window, I got up to check to see if any of my neighbors had their headlights on, but they didn't. I have always thought that it was an orb."

For daughter Kaitlyn, her first experience would be a bit more obvious and convincing than that, as she awoke in the middle of the night to see a ghost standing next to the bed that her two sisters were sharing.

"I looked over and I noticed that there was a woman standing next to their bed. She was pure white, with long dark hair and she was wearing a gown. It was the first time that I had ever seen a ghost. You would think that I would have been scared, but I wasn't. I sat up in bed and we looked at each other. For some reason, I had the notion to stand up. So I swung my legs off the side of the bed, but as soon as my feet hit the floor, she disappeared into my sisters' headboard. I went back to bed, pulled the covers over my head and fell back to sleep. It wasn't until the morning that I realized how surreal and unbelievable that was. And yet, something about her appearance had felt calming to me. I remember telling my mom about it and she said that it sounded like a ghost that my brother had seen just a few weeks prior."

For Rose and her husband Scott, things would continue to be perplexing and at times annoying. But as we will see, the situation was about to get downright terrifying for Kaitlyn and her two sisters.

"One night, my husband and I went upstairs to bed," said Rose, "and we heard someone coming up the stairs. My husband got out of bed and turned the hallway light on to check, but there was nothing there, so he went back to bed. Then we heard it again. It was definitely the sound of footsteps coming up the stairs. This time he waited until it got to the top of the stairs, then he ran out into the hallway, real fast. There was still nothing there. He checked the children. They were in their beds, sound asleep."

"At night, it would always sound like someone was walking up the stairs," daughter Shannon concurred. "It creaked a lot.

And when you would be going up the stairs yourself, you always got the feeling that someone was following you up."

Holly agreed with that assessment. Numerous were the times when her petrified three year old son Xzavier would come to her to tell her about the creepy old man in the top hat standing at the top of the stairs.

On a separate occasion, it seemed as though whatever was climbing the stairs after the family had retired for the evening, was also trying to climb into the bed with the couple.

"There was another time when I was in bed sleeping, and I woke up to the feeling that someone was crawling up along the side of me. It started from the foot of the bed. I jumped up and put the light on, but there was nothing there. And this happened a few times."

When it wasn't the disincorporated footsteps on the stairs driving the couple crazy with exasperation, it was the noises coming from outside pulling Scott out of bed in the middle of the night to investigate.

"We also experienced frequent banging on our windows, and when you looked out, there was nothing there to explain it. My husband would run out with a flashlight and look around the whole yard, but he would never find anything. At the time there was nothing behind us or on the side of the house but woods. Miles and miles of woods."

Unbeknownst to their parents, the girls were catching glimpses here and there of glowing red eyes, peering through the windows at night. Meanwhile, down the hall, in the bedroom where her daughters were sleeping, the three girls were being subjected to something even more sinister than peeping eyes and things going *Bump* in the night.

"One night when I was young, I felt something crawling on me," recalled Shannon. "It felt like there was a cat kneading on me, so I cried out to my sister Holly. She told me that there was a woman standing next to my bed and three cats on top of me. I felt like I couldn't breathe. I kept telling the woman to leave, then I asked Holly to tell her. I know that this is going to sound crazy," she continued, transitioning to another story, "but when we were kids my grandmother had made my sister Kaitlyn a doll with hair made out of long blue yarn. There was one time when I was laying in the bottom bunk and the doll fell through the space between the bed and the wall and got stuck, so that its legs were still pinned to the wall by the top bunk, but the head and the rest of the body had fallen through to the bottom. After it fell, its head was facing me and I heard it say 'BOO' in a deep, demonic voice. I screamed, then I grabbed the doll and threw it into the closet."

As bad as having the demonic Chatty Cathy dropping in for a scare had been, things were about to get much worse for twin sisters Shannon and Holly.

"Holly and I had beds that were across from each other, and our younger sister slept on the other side of the room. One night, we both saw this demonic-looking creature appear between our two beds," recalled Shannon. "It had large, pointed teeth, big ears and dark eyes that bugged out, and it was hopping like a bunny, back and forth between our beds. Our dad yelled up to ask us what was going on. When he started walking up the stairs, Holly got the courage to run to the light that was close to the entrance, and as she did, the creature chased after her. Once my dad got to the room and switched the light on, the creature disappeared."

"I remember that so clearly," said Holly. "It was pretty scary. I also remember this one time when I was in my bed, and I had this immense amount of fear, to the point where I couldn't move. I tried to yell for my parents but it was hard for me to get the words out. I would manage to say *mom,* but it wasn't loud enough to be heard. My words were like a whisper because I was so terrified. I didn't see anything, but I felt horrible, like something was with me, but I just couldn't see it. I don't remember how it managed to stop, but I will never forget that feeling."

"That would happen to me too," said Shannon. "I would feel almost paralyzed. I couldn't yell at all."

It is referenced in religion, mythology, folklore and depicted in popular media that demons have the ability to shape-shift, which includes appearing in the form of an animal. It is probably by no small measure of coincidence that the demon that had shown itself to the two girls had taken on the grotesque and exaggerated features of an animal usually considered to be soft, cuddly and harmless in order to exert a maximum amount of terror in the sisters, and this is partially what set the Miller Street address apart from other hauntings in the area. That wasn't a ghost. That was a demon. The family was dealing with harmless apparitions, orbs, strange noises, shadow people and a decidedly evil presence. Nobody else that I talked to in the area had that kind of a combination to contend with. Again, the only thing comparable to it was what had occurred at the Conjuring House in the 1970's.

When I conducted my interview with Devon, he had mentioned to me that he always had a weird feeling in the house, particularly upstairs. It was his brother who confirmed the notion, saying that he believed that the evil spirits seemed to be concentrated in his sisters' bedroom. And while he may have been sympathetic to their nightly plight of terrors, Shane and his younger brothers would end up getting an up close and personal look at exactly what they had been dealing with.

"There were definitely two spirits in the house," he said. "A nice one, which was like a younger kid, who'd I'd seen and wasn't afraid of at all. But the other one was terrifying. I think that the evil one was in the bigger bedroom, because the girls had that room first. When Devin was born, we switched bedrooms because after that the boys outnumbered the girls. Growing up, I shared that room with my two younger brothers. We had a bunk bed in there and a regular bed. The dog usually slept under mine. One night, I woke up to the sound of the television turning on by itself, with it displaying just static. Then I heard a low growl coming from under the bed. Half asleep, I told the dog to be quiet, but it didn't stop. Annoyed, I leaned over to look under the bed just to find out that the dog wasn't there, or even in the room. I woke up my brothers, but as soon as I did that the noise just stopped. I often heard that growl, or someone saying my name. Anytime you were in that room, or even upstairs in general, you could just feel a different energy at times. The room felt colder and it gave you anxiety, the hairs would stand up like goosebumps."

Just like all of his siblings, middle brother Dillon also had things in the bedroom keeping him awake and making it hard to sleep at night.

"The first thing that I ever physically saw was back when I was in middle school in 2008. It was a summer night and I had the windows open. Devin was sleeping over at a friend's house. I remember waking up at a really odd hour, like two or three in the morning, and there was this huge ball of light in my room. I rubbed my eyes, thinking that I was just sleepy, then I realized that it was a real, pulsating ball of light sitting in between the two bedroom windows. It was about the size of a volleyball, just like this soft white/orange ball of light that seemed to hover over my TV. The strangest part was that it didn't illuminate anything around it and even though it looked bright, it didn't hurt your eyes to look at it. I remember being afraid and thinking that maybe I should make a run for it, because the door was behind me, but I was too scared. So I decided to just hide under the covers."

"A few years after my first encounter," continued Dillon, "I was having anxiety one night and I couldn't sleep. So I decided to go downstairs, where I sat on the couch and watched TV. My dad was snoring on the couch, but he'd had some 1970's sitcom TV show on. I think it was TV Land, or something. I kept watching it for a while, and then I caught something out of the corner of my eye. I looked to see what it was, and a toddler was standing there. It was a boy, he couldn't have been more than three years old. He ran by me and then proceeded across the room. Then he dropped down on both knees, and he was looking at an old wooden toy horse that he had in his hands. He looked over at my father, who was still sleeping on the couch, then he just dissipated in front of my eyes. It was a little white boy, with dirty blond, curly hair.

He was wearing a cloth diaper, and he didn't make a sound as he passed by. He wasn't whitish, like you think of a ghost being. He was the color of human skin, except shadowy and transparent, like a photo that's been photoshopped. At first, it confused me because I thought it might be my nephew Xzavier. But he was in the other room, sleeping."

Like his brother Devon, Dillon had also been alarmed at times by the sound of hearing the vent grate crashing into their bedroom door.

"We had this floor vent on top of our stairs that took some effort to take out of the floor, it was fairly heavy. There were a few times when me and my brothers would be in our room and we would hear a loud crash at the door, only to find that same vent grate on the floor, right in the doorway where it had landed. Somehow, the vent grate was picked up out of the floor, went around a corner and still had enough force to hit our door."

Said mom Rose of the strange event: "At the top of the hallway staircase we have a heat vent in the floor, which is removable, but it is heavy and seated tightly in the floor. On this particular day, our Neapolitan mastiff was lying in the hallway upstairs when we heard a loud bang. We ran upstairs and the dog was trembling. The floor vent was out of the floor and against the bedroom door as if someone had thrown it. This happened numerous times, and we were not running the furnace at the time that any of these events occurred."

And yet, the heating vent grate wasn't the only thing moving about the house, seemingly under its own power.

"We had an incident once when it was only me and my husband at home," said Rose. "We were in the living room watching TV when we heard a crash in the kitchen. The heater that was plugged in on the counter was on the floor as if someone had deliberately knocked it off."

Sometimes Rose will be in the kitchen washing dishes and she thinks she hears someone walking across the kitchen floor. When she looks, no one is there.

"Just the other night, I felt someone touch my hair. I thought that it was my husband coming up behind me to put his hand on my shoulder. I turned around quickly, but no one was there."

At other times, the family is perplexed by the distinct smell of cigarette smoke wafting through the home. Curious because no one in the family smokes.

"It happens at all different times of the year," said Rose. "It doesn't matter if the windows are open or closed, we still smell it.

As we have already discussed, dogs have no trouble seeing ghosts, because their rod-dominant eyes can readily pick things up manifesting lower on the spectrum of visible light. On Miller Street, Buddy, the family's Neapolitan mastiff, could sometimes be seen reacting to strange occurrences that no one else could see.

"One night, my husband, the kids and I were all sitting in the living room, and there was a quick, cold draft that came through the house. Well, Buddy started growling and looking towards the staircase in the hallway. He watched whatever it was, as if someone was walking past and into the next room. He never got up, he just growled and watched. It was kind of eerie."

Most of the time however, you didn't need the heightened senses of a canine to see and hear the phenomena that was occurring all around, and on a regular basis. Like the times when the house made such a loud noise that it seemed as though it might collapse.

"One day, we were all sitting in my parent's living room. It was Easter, about six or seven years ago," recalled Shannon, " and all of a sudden we heard a huge bang, like someone had dropped a huge weight on top of the house. We all ran out outside, thinking that it was going to collapse. My dad and brother looked around the house and in the basement, and checked out the beams and joists. There was nothing visibly wrong."

"This also happened again, a few years later," said Rose. "I was having a washer and dryer delivered and the delivery men were in the middle of carrying the washer in, when a loud *bang!* caused them to release the washer from their belts and start running towards the door. I had to stop them from leaving and assure them that it was okay, that it had happened before and that there was actually nothing wrong."

*Nothing wrong* was a term used loosely in the family's Miller Street home, and one that Shannon's son, Brayden, might wholeheartedly disagree with. He lived with his grandparents while attending high school in the area.

"I had one encounter with an orb while I was there that was different and scary," he said. "I had a friend sleeping over, and it was probably ten or eleven o'clock at night. I decided to go downstairs to grab a couple of drinks. When I came back to the stairs, I would normally sprint up them because there was always this feeling like you were going to get chased by something from behind. But before I did that, I looked to the top of the stairwell, and I saw a black orb just floating there at the top. It wasn't a glowing bright light, like we would normally see around the house, it was dark. So I tried to ignore it and run up anyway, but when I did that and got to the top of the stairs, it flew off and stopped for a second at each of the three bedroom doors, mine was last. As I went to run into the room, it flew directly into my chest. It didn't hurt or anything, but it kind of just felt like this extra added weight that felt weird. I asked my friend if I looked okay, and he said that I looked pale. So I grabbed a crucifix off the wall, held it to my chest and prayed. That was the most terrifying thing that I experienced without any of the family there."

In consideration of the extent of the supernatural activity going on in the house, I asked Rose if the family had ever thought about selling the house and moving away.

"No, we never considered selling the house," said Rose. "In all reality, we had a house full of kids and could not have financially afforded to move even if we wanted to. No one was ever physically hurt by any of the events. Yes, we knew that something was here and did talk about maybe having someone come in to check out the paranormal activity. But we decided that as long as no one was being harmed that we would just have to live with it."

Like a few of the houses that I've written about so far, the house on Miller Street had a past that included people dying inside the home itself. The family had purchased the property from a couple by the name of Joseph and Clara. They had two children, Helen and Joe Jr. The younger Joseph was a veteran of the Korean War who had returned from active duty with PTSD. He would live with his parents for the rest of his life, which ended from a heart attack as he was standing in the kitchen, looking out the window. The father would die on his bedroom floor, after being found next to his bed, in what would later become the living room. Daughter Helen and her husband Walter lived in a cottage on the property that Rose and family later turned into a shed. While it is possible that these deaths, along with the negative energy from the younger Joe's condition, exacerbated the supernatural activity that was witnessed later on, it is true that those houses that seemed to be the most active had all seen multiple deaths occur inside the home itself, and while those deaths alone do not appear to be the source of the paranormal activity taken as a whole, it does seem to be a contributing factor, although it does not entirely explain the dozens of hauntings known to be occurring roughly between Main Street in Millville, and Main Street in Harrisville, Rhode Island. I stand convinced that the phenomenon as a whole in this area is being generated and sustained by a geological feature, such as an electromagnetic field resulting from an underground flow of water. It seems reasonable to conclude that when a person dies that a portal of sorts must open between this plane of existence and the next, since there must be a way for the soul to move between here and the afterlife once the body is deceased. The question then becomes one of trying to explain how so many hauntings can be taking place over such a short distance specific to this particular stretch of land. Is it possible that the catalyst that is allowing this paranormal activity to take place is propping  open the end of life portals that should be closing after the transfer of a soul from here to there? Or is it simply poking holes in whatever it is that separates the two, allowing the recently deceased or even the long dead to move between planes of existence, simply because they can? The evidence suggests that at the very least, the option to do so clearly exists.

**The Miller Street address is one of the most haunted locations in the town of Millville. Note how close it is to the "Demon House" on Chesley Street. It is also near the Blackstone Valley Greenway Bike Path haunted by "Lucy on the Lock." That's Hope Street behind the bike path, with its two hauntings. West Street is just above and to the left of Hope Street, with at least three more hauntings of its own. Courtesy of Google Maps.**

C hapter 19: The Main Problem

I wasn't surprised when Jackie reached out to tell me about her house on Main Street. The area down on Main is haunted as hell and I had already had discussions with people about what was happening at the pub. Across the street and over by Preston, is a house where LJ told me that the ghost of an old woman can be seen sitting in a chair on the front porch, rocking back and forth, a haunting later confirmed to me by Shawna. Her mom's friend had once owned that house, and many ghost stories had circulated about the place when she was a child. As an adult, Shawna would later believe that she saw the apparition of a child looking out the first floor window, and what appeared to be a woman in Victorian clothing standing in front of a window on the second. Could this be the old woman that others have seen rocking on the front porch? It was also LJ who told me about the big house no on Main, across the street from the pub. Then another Jackie, this one on Preston Street, right near the ghostly rocker, reached out to tell me that she awoke every morning to the sound of footsteps in the empty upstairs.

"Two people had previously died in that house," she told me, of the place that she called home for fourteen years. Once her children moved their bedrooms to the second floor, the strange noises stopped.

Now another Jackie was reaching out to tell me about another haunted house on Main, this one up past the library as you're driving out of town. This would make five such hauntings in less than a quarter mile of highway. What are the odds of that?

**Five different hauntings have been reported on Main Street. The pub is said to be haunted, as well as a house across the street, a house next to Preston Street and down the street itself, and also near the library, which was once a train station. Just a coincidence? Courtesy of Google Maps.**

Jackie and family moved into the house on Main Street in 2000. And for several years, nothing strange or unusual happened. It wasn't until her youngest child reached the ages of five or six that things began to change inside the home.

"We began to see the spirit of a little girl moving about the house," recalled Jackie. "She was about five or six years old. It coincided with when my youngest was about the same age as the spirit. It lasted from about 2007 until 2010. During this time, we would see her peeking around door frames or hear her running in the upstairs hallway, even though my kids were asleep. She was wearing a long nightgown. There was one occasion where I saw a bottle of perfume fly off my bureau."

Separately, a friend of the family once stood witness as an accordion door shook violently for a full minute, and without any apparent explanation.

The house, which was built in 1850, may have once served as the local sheriff's residence and possibly the county lockup, according to an oral history that Jackie recalled hearing.

"There's a rectangular room in the basement that looks like it was a jail cell," she noted.

According to L. Clement, of the Millville Historical Commission, Town Hall once occupied the land across the street from where the house currently sits. Criminals would be taken to the police station housed on the first floor, in order to be booked and processed, before being shipped to Blackstone, because Millville itself did not have its own jail at the time. It makes sense that the sheriff may have lived in the house across the street from the police station, and that there may have been a holding cell in the basement for felons awaiting transport to Blackstone, but I was not definitively able to prove that.

As far as the little ghost girl is concerned, she appeared to lose interest in showing herself after Jackie's kids aged out of the spirit's own eternal age, perhaps suggesting that the spirit may have manifested in the first place so that it could play and/or interact with what it perceived to be peers. But Jackie occasionally thinks to this day that she can still see things moving about the house from the corner of her eye. When she looks, there is nothing there. Gone since 2010, the little ghost girl isn't the only spirit the family has seen on the property. As recently as 2021, Jackie's brother-in-law said he saw the image of a tall, older man wearing a top hat and a suit with tails standing in the middle of the family's front driveway.

"He was translucent, but colorful at the same time," I was told.

The fashion would have been something that people wore beginning in 1800 until the end of the nineteenth century. It was especially popular around 1850, when it became a symbol of urban respectability, courtesy of an endorsement by Prince Albert, a member of the royal family in England at the time. This also fits into the timeline for when the home was constructed. Originally, it sat next door to the Main Street train station. Could it be that the spirit in top hat and tails was standing in wait to catch a train? The ghost train perhaps?

C hapter 20: Meanwhile, on Chestnut Hill RD

At this point, would it really be surprising to anyone to learn that there are not one, but at least three different hauntings occurring up on Chestnut Hill Road? And those are just the ones that I know about!

Patricia was the second person to reach out to me from Chestnut Hill, but unfortunately, she was the only one to grant me an interview.

"My mom's house does some weird things!" she teased, in response to a post that I'd made on a local social-media site.

Like some of the paranormal encounters that I've covered so far, such as the Kempton Road haunting or the one on Preston Street, the activity that Pat's mom has experienced at this particular location falls more into the category of being a subtle accumulation of strange events, spaced out here and there over a long period of time. This includes both occurrences that defy a satisfactory explanation, and noises generated without any real identifiable cause.

To be clear, there have been no bloody back scratches or angry entities reported at this particular address. No streaks of energy crashing through the house and destroying keepsakes and closets, like over on West Street. Nor have there been any heavy objects flying through the house and crashing into doors and pets, like on Miller Street. There have also (thankfully) been no scary as hell red-eyed shadow people lurking around outside and looking in windows, like at both of those aforementioned locations. No, this Chestnut Hill haunting has been defined, at least so far, by a proclivity for the less dramatic. But that doesn't make it any less interesting, or what happened to Pat's mom and her partner any less important in the grand scheme of things regarding the overall picture. Millville is one of the most haunted places around, and this is a story about that, as much as it is about anything else. Let's take a look at some of the things that have been happening.

For Pat's mom, the questions began soon after moving into the Chestnut Hill Road address to live with her longtime partner.

"He owns the house," Pat told me, "and has lived there a lot longer than my mom. They've been together for a long time. The house was built in 1945, so I think that weird stuff has been happening there for a while now."

It began with mom being perplexed over the sound of the garage door opening in the afternoon. Thinking that it was her partner coming home from work, she wondered why she hadn't heard him pull into the driveway. As a man with a penchant for riding his motorcycle, it should have been obvious. But it wasn't him at all. Whenever she went to check, no one was there, the door having opened by itself. Thinking that it may be some kind of electrical short, I asked Pat if it was connected to a motorized garage door opener.

"It is," she told me. "But it hasn't been hooked up to the electricity yet. They have to open and close it manually."

Like so many other houses in town, the couple have also been hearing noises coming from the attic that shouldn't be there. Footsteps when no one is upstairs, going back and forth and round and round. Banging noises, the sound of things being moved around, as if someone is rearranging the furniture. Most persistent and recent to the penning of this chapter has been the sound of a ball rolling as it goes across the floor from one side of the attic to the other. Even stranger is the fact that when Pat's mother goes upstairs to investigate, the mysterious ball is nowhere to be found.

"For the last two months my mom has been hearing the sound of a golf ball rolling around in the attic," Pat told me. "What's weird about it is that nothing has ever rolled around up there before. And what's even weirder is that she can never find the golf ball when she goes upstairs to look for it. The floor isn't exactly flat, so she doesn't know why or how this is happening.

My sister was the one who found it when she went up there just the other day. But this was something new, it hadn't happened before."

Meanwhile downstairs, doors throughout the home have been seen to open and close on their own volition and with no apparent explanation to account for the movement. And on top of that, the lights in the house flicker at night in a strange manner, as if the power is going to go out, but in a way that seems unnatural for a common outage.

To be sure, there are legitimate explanations for why this could be happening, such as power grid surges, drawing too much juice from the circuit box, and faulty or old wiring. But if that's the case, then who's opening and closing all the doors and making all that noise in the attic? Is that the house's electrical system too?

Some paranormal researchers have suggested that ghosts may dim the lights as a means to interact with the physical world, in order to get our attention. But it is more likely that ghosts and spirits are either composed entirely of electromagnetic energy, or at the very least, they are using it to help manifest an appearance. Remember that electromagnetic energy fields have been implicated as a catalyst for time slips, paranormal encounters of all kinds and the replaying of images, sounds and physical impressions imprinted on the fabric of time. Lights, television and radio waves all use a version of this kind of energy to function. It is therefore reasonable to conclude that when a ghost is present, it may disrupt the electricity being used to power lights, appliances and the like because it is siphoning off some of that energy to maintain its presence in this plane of existence. It is also possible that the electromagnetic energy field that accompanies the manifestation is simply causing a disturbance in the  normal flow of electricity through the home's wiring and connections, in much the same way that overlapping radio stations cancel each other out, so that neither can be clearly heard. In any event, there is a resident ghost in the house. And her name is Mary. One night as the couple were sitting outside, she decided to make an appearance.

"They were outside one night by the fire," Pat told me. "And they saw a woman's face looking out a window. Nobody was in the house at the time."

I asked Pat why the couple refer to the ghost woman as "Mary," but she wasn't sure where the moniker came from. Perhaps Mary was looking out the window because she was wondering who left all the lights on.

C hapter 21: Central to the Argument

Assume the position in a comfortable spot of repose and silence your cell phone. Send the kids to bed early if you need to and clear your schedule, because this one is going to get interesting.

Time was in the small town of Millville that if you wanted to see for yourself the kind of wealth, privilege and opportunity that the mill industry was bringing to the area, that you needed to look no further than as to what was happening over on Central Street. Wide open farm land at the turn of the nineteenth-century, the Industrial Revolution had turned that neighborhood into a showcase for all of the beautiful homes that were being constructed by both the mill owners themselves, as well as the people who ran them. This included my own grandfather, who was acting president of Stanley Woolen Mills and had settled in at 83 Central to raise a family with his wife Ethel. The home, which had been built in 1825, sat on nine acres of land and boasted seven bedrooms, four bathrooms and fifteen rooms in total within its 5,000 square feet of living space. There was also a guest house attached to the main house which added an additional 4,500 square feet to the estate. A barn with horse stables and a carriage house was attached to the guest house. A detached three car garage sat at the end of the driveway. The property, which fronted Central Street on Smyth Curve, was originally lined by large pine trees and surrounded by a white picket fence, which enclosed a spacious lawn that climbed into a hill in back that had a concrete pool set into the top of it, with a screened pool house sitting in the very back. On the other side of the pool and the pool house was a thick tangle of woods, but to the left of the hill and next to the garage there was a dirt trail that led to a pond that was stocked with fish. When the upkeep and tax burden got too sizable for my uncle Harrison's widow to manage, she sold the property to a developer who first parceled out half of the land and then split the house and attached structures into two distinct residences (condo-style) now identified as 83 and 85 Central Street, totaling 9,700 square feet and containing a total of 14 bedrooms and 9 bathrooms. Was it haunted? My mom always said that it was, and a cousin who grew up in the house agreed. They both remembered the sound of someone traversing the stairs when there was no one there.

"There was always someone walking around that house," my cousin (who asked to remain anonymous) said. "My dad got out of bed one night, and he was ready to clobber whoever it was that was coming up the stairs. But nobody was there. My mom once told me that as she and my dad were sitting at the kitchen table, the pull-string on the light went flying as if someone had flicked it with their finger. Grandma used to yell at me all the time for getting up in the middle of the night and leaving the water on in the bathroom. She never believed me when I told her that I hadn't been in the bathroom."

"There were many times when I was alone in that house," said another Smyth cousin, "and swear there was someone in the house with me."

For the record, I never saw or heard anything to support the claim of a haunting there myself. But I only visited once a year and I was very young at the time. We slept at West Street and mostly limited our time at the Central Street address so day visits.

Meanwhile, down the street and closer to Banigan's City, another Irish immigrant by the name of James Alexander Kidd was busy putting his own mill-gotten gains to work, by erecting a house for himself and his family in 1900. Less than half the size of my grandfather's place, this house had 12 rooms, which included six bedrooms and servant's quarters spread throughout a total of just over 2,000 square feet. Out back stood a two-story, three car garage/carriage house, next to a two seat outhouse that is still there to this very day.

James Kidd was born on October 22, 1835 in Bovevaugh County, Londonderry, Ireland. He arrived in New York City on June 15, 1868 at the age of 32, before eventually making his way north to the small town of Millville, Massachusetts, which was at the time just an unincorporated village of Blackstone. He petitioned to become a Naturalized citizen on October 27, 1868, less than a week past his 33rd birthday. Once settled in the region with his citizenship in hand, he assumed control of the old Mansfield Scythe Works and converted it into a woolens manufacturer under the name of Booth and Kidd. He died on March 16, 1909 at the age of 72 in Blackstone, Massachusetts. Sometime before his death, he moved west of Millville with his wife Margaret and sold the house to yet another local mill owner by the name of John Mahoney and his wife Ellen.

As a prominent and wealthy local family of Irish catholic descent, the Mahoney's would sometimes play host to members of the politically influential Kennedy family, who would occasionally stay over at the Central Street address, which was at the time just a two-minute walk to the nearest train station. They would raise six children in the house, pairing three sons to go along with three daughters. Oddly enough, none of their six children would have any children of their own, and the three girls would all go on to become spinsters, never marrying and spending their whole lives in the family home, while working as teachers in the local school system. Also unusual for the time was the fact that all three women were college educated, in an era in which only 7% of females received a higher education. Youngest daughter Anna would go on to attend Wellesley College, where she became fast friends with Soong Mei-Ling, who would herself later go on to marry Chiang Kai-Shek in 1927, the last President of Nationalist China. Mei-Ling, who would one day be the future First Lady of Taiwan, would come to Millville to visit with Anna, staying at the Central Street home on numerous occasions. Perhaps owing to the influence of this friendship, one of the rooms in the house had been specifically decorated with wallpaper styled after Chinese patterns, beneath which lie a red carpet, a symbol of good luck in China. It was here where the women would converse in the afternoon, while enjoying each other's company over a pot of tea. The daughter of a wealthy Chinese businessman, it was said that Mei-Ling required the bed linens and pillow cases to be changed out each day during her stay.

The second youngest of the Mahoney children, Anna outlived all of her siblings by a minimum of twenty-six years, with middle sister Helen going first, passing away inside the house in 1947, while older sister Mary followed suit twenty years later in 1967.

**The Mahoney family sitting for a family portrait circa 1905. Pictured are Ellen, John Jr, Mary, Helen, Anna, John, Joseph and Walter. Photo courtesy of D. Drewniak.**

Anna would live to the ripe old age of 94, having spent most of those years calling the Central Street address her home. In 1991, she moved into a skilled nursing care facility, where she lived out the remainder of her long life. The following year, the property came under fire literally, when two teenage boys burned the carriage house to the ground and attempted to burn the house down with it by lighting a fire on the cellar stairs, reputedly because they thought that the property belonged to a local police officer with whom they held a grudge. The officer had indeed been storing a boat in Anna's carriage house, but had moved it out only a week before the fire was set. After sitting empty for over a year, the house was eventually put up for sale, and this is where Dave and his wife Anna enter the picture.

As soon as the couple moved to Central Street, they had their work cut out for them. The house was outdated and nearly one-hundred years old. It had also sat empty and unoccupied for close to a year, with the only exception being the unwelcomed visit by the two would-be arsonists. Renovations began room by room just two short weeks after they took possession of the property, and that's when Dave told me that strange things began to happen in the house. It started, as it so often does, with unexplained noises coming forth from empty rooms.

"I woke up one morning," he told me, "and I thought that I heard people talking downstairs. It was sometime between one o'clock and three in the morning. The way the house is laid out there are four bedrooms on the second floor spaced around a walkway leading to the stairs. You can look down from it and see the doorways below, but you can't see into the rooms. I got up out of bed, walked to the stairway and leaned over it. I could clearly hear two women speaking with each other. I couldn't make out what they were saying, but I could specifically hear that they were sipping and drinking tea. It was so distinct that I could hear the sound of the sugar grinding as they were stirring it into their porcelain tea cups with a spoon. It gave me chills as I stood there listening to it, so I turned around and went back to bed. The next morning, I asked my wife if she'd heard it, but she said that he hadn't. This happened three or four times over the course of about a year or so, and then we never heard it again."

In need of more convincing than just the post-midnight tea party that in Anna's mind could have just as easily been a dream, Dave's claim of hearing things in the downstairs parlor at night would eventually find some validation when Anna herself began getting the occasional thank you for doing things that she had not actually done.

"I had my two young nieces that would have sleepovers at the house sometimes, and they would wake up the next morning and thank my wife for tucking them in the night before, only she hadn't. She never got out of bed to check on them. She acknowledged the appreciation, but she didn't tell them that it wasn't her."

When questioned, the girls each said that a woman dressed in a white bathrobe had come into their room the night before and had tucked them into bed. No one in the house fit that description, with Anna and her husband Dave being the only two people home with the girls at the time.

"And this happened several times," Dave added, noting that his wife later confessed that she had indeed heard the voices coming from the old tea room at night.

Not long after they had moved in, an older woman who was passing by the property stopped by to speak to the couple as they were outside doing yard work. She told them that Anna Murphy used to have tea in the downstairs parlor and asked whether or not they had heard the voices coming from the old tea room, to which Dave acknowledged that they had.

Meanwhile, at night Dave was also being woken up as he slept by the distinct impression that someone was coming down the hall and walking past his bedroom door.

"There were times when I'd be lying in bed, and the doorway is to the right of me, I'd get a feeling as if somebody had just walked by. So I would look, but I never caught a glimpse of anybody, but there was always this feeling as if something had been there."

Like many of the hauntings in town, the paranormal activity that occurred at the Central Street address was spaced out over a length of time between encounters and ultimately ephemeral when compared to the couple's thirty-plus years of residency. According to Dave, the strange things that the couple both saw and heard happened during the first three years that they lived there, then just stopped altogether.

"The last encounter that we ever had," recalled Dave, "my wife was in the house alone, and it was like one or two o'clock in the afternoon. She was at the kitchen sink, washing dishes and she heard her name being called. *Anna? Anna?* So she turned around and said 'what?' Then she called out to her mother, thinking that she had come into the house through the front door, but that was odd because that door is always locked. The kitchen is in the back, and that's the entrance that we use. Then she realized that she was in the house by herself. And this happened just before Anna Mahoney passed away."

But was the spirit calling out to Anna the housewife, or Anna Mahoney? Was it even a spirit at all? Perhaps it was the sound of Anna Mahoney's own mother calling to her as she had once done in the house, imprinted on the fabric of time and being replayed as if it were happening in the now. Is it a coincidence that Anna Mahoney died soon after this happened? Maybe it was the voice of one of her sisters calling out because they were expecting her company in the afterlife.

Who knows?

After the couple purchased the house in May of 1993, Anna Mahoney had reached out to them and asked if they would come see her.

"She was in a nursing home at that point. We had dealt with her niece, Millie Mahoney, all through the closing. Anna wasn't getting a dime from the sale of the property, it was all going to the nursing home. But she had asked Millie a number of times if we would go up to meet with her. I work six days a week, so that meant that Sunday was the only day where we would be able to go up to the nursing home to visit. The Friday before we were scheduled to go, I opened up the Woonsocket Call that morning and her obituary was in the paper. We didn't know that she had contracted pneumonia, and because she was so old, she died of it. But we always have felt that we are the caretakers of this house, that it's still the Mahoney home and that I'm just here taking care of it for them. It's a very odd feeling."

So, what does Dave think about his experiences in the house all these years after they happened?

"The encounters that we had were not threatening. They weren't scary to the degree where it was like *Get out, Get out*. It's just what it was. It's as simple as that."

**Central Street can be seen running through the center of town. Note the proximity to hauntings on West Street, Hope Street, Ironstone Street and The Lock. Courtesy of Google Maps.**

C hapter 22: The Old Ghost Home

When Kerrie reached out to me to say that her parents had owned a nursing home on Central Street and that she "guaranteed" that it was one of the most haunted places in town, I knew exactly what she was talking about.

"I think that my mom worked at that nursing home back in the 1950's," I said, figuring that it must be the same one. I mean, how many old folks homes had there ever been on Central Street?

"It was called Cullen's Nursing Home," she replied. "My parents owned it all the way up into the 1970's, before closing the doors. We lived there for a while."

"Yes, that's the one," I answered back. "I recognize the name. My mom worked there in the latter part of the 1950's and into the early half of the 1960's. She always used to say that it was haunted whenever she mentioned it."

Joseph and Irene Cullen originally purchased the beautiful 4,600 square foot house back in 1956, before turning the one-time private residence into a nursing home. The house itself dated to 1900.

"It originally had a library and servants quarters," said Kerrie. "There were many beautiful and ornate fireplaces inside as well. It was said that there were underground tunnels running from house to house, to and from next door and the place across the street."

She didn't know it, but my grandfather had once owned the house across the street, the estate beginning at 83 Central. The old nursing home sat directly across from my grandfather's backyard. It was interesting to hear her mention the tunnels, because when my uncle Harrison's widow sold the estate in the early part of the 2000's, the realtor had added to the description of the home and property that it had once served as a stop on the Underground Railroad, a detail that I had never once heard mentioned by anyone, and a fact that I'd found curious since generations of the Smyth family had owned the estate for eighty-something years. To be fair, nobody ever talked about the relation to President Garfield either. An aunt who was into genealogy had included it in a family history that she'd sent to me. So maybe none of that stuff was considered particularly interesting or important. I don't know. The fact that there were supposedly tunnels running between each house, and that Kerrie had heard the stories from her side of Central Street as well, lent credence to the possibility that it might have been true after all. The only thing throwing a monkey wrench into that whole theory was the fact that the nursing home and neighboring houses were all built long after slavery had ended. My grandfather's house dated to 1825, so that made sense, but not the tunnels to houses that wouldn't be built for 30-40 years after the fact. It's possible that those newer houses had been built on top of civil war era structures that had since been demolished, but again, I don't know.

When she first told me that she had an association to "the most haunted home" in Millville, I was both intrigued and dubious all at the same time. Intrigued because...well, why not? And dubious because I already knew about the demon house on Chesley Street, as well as all the crazy stuff that had been going on over on Miller. Even West Street had experienced moments of aggressively negative energy. So let's just say that I had my doubts. Still, I was hoping for a good story. Like West Street, I knew from what my mom had said, that this particular haunting had been going on for a long time, so the potential was certainly there.

One of the things that has stuck with Kerrie these fifty-years after the fact is the feeling that she got from the basement. Housing the facility's laundry room, she had a need for going down there on a regular basis, and she hated it.

"I couldn't go down there alone," she recalled. "The basement had the worst feeling about it, and sometimes you couldn't even get down there because the door would lock shut, even though there wasn't an actual lock on it. That's where the highest feeling of the presence of spirits was. Luckily, some of our higher functioning patients would help out with the laundry, so I didn't always have to go down there by myself."

"Was there any reason for the spirits to be specifically concentrated in the basement?" I asked. Thinking of West Street, and the wakes that had been held in the front bedroom, I wondered if residents who passed away had been held in the basement pending removal to a funeral home.

"I'm not sure," answered Kerrie. "As far as I know, we never stored dead bodies down there."

Making the rounds between floors, including the basement, was the facility's dumb-waiter, which would go up and down between the house's different levels without any explanation or prompting from an employee or resident.

"It would make the hair stand up on the back of your neck," noted Kerrie, who could also remember hearing footsteps in the attic when no one was up there and muffled voices coming from the empty rooms below.

"There was a room in the attic that was used for storage, but it had a functional toilet as well. Most of the footsteps seemed to come from that area. On the floor below, you could always hear the sounds of someone mumbling."

Meanwhile, down in the first floor kitchen, staff regularly had a difficult time keeping the meal prep area organized, as paper towels were constantly being unrolled from the rack upon which they sat.

Unfortunately, that's where the story ends. Perhaps relying on a memory that was fifty or sixty years long on the details, that's all the information that I got about the old nursing home on Central Street. I'm certain that if my mom was still alive that she would have had plenty of stories of her own. But she passed away during the Covid 19 lockdown. Ironically, while living under quarantine in a nursing home. The same kind of institution where she has spent the majority of her adult life working for a living.

C hapter 23: The Demon House on Chesley Street

It wasn't until I sat down with my cousin Richard to discuss the renovation of our two-family rental unit in Worcester county that I even got an inkling that there might be other hauntings occurring in the town of Millville. The thought had never occurred to me. I had no idea that my grandmother's house on West Street was nothing special. I had no idea whatsoever how big and widespread the situation really was. Then Rich mentioned Chesley Street, and it was off to the races. Turns out that the house on West Street is just one of at least two dozen hauntings all taking place in the same general area. And to think that it all started with a throwaway statement that my wife made about Rich's peculiar living arrangement.

"So, you live in the house with all the ghosts," she said.

"Geez," he responded, shaking his head in the negative, beneath the huff of a subtle laugh, surprised and probably not accustomed to getting hit with a conversation starter like that. "You don't even know," he said.

For years, I had shared dribs and drabs with her regarding my own paranormal experiences there. But she wasn't a believer, having never seen anything of the like herself, and thus having no foundation to base an understanding on. Now, Rich was feeding her stories that were even harder to believe than anything that I had ever said.

As I sat across the table from him and listened to stories that even I didn't know, my wheels began to turn.

"There's a lot of meat on that bone," I offered. "That would be a good book."

That's when the subject of the house on Chesley Street came up, and I was like...'what?'

"You're saying that there's another house nearby West Street that is haunted as well?" I asked.

"Not just haunted," said Rich. "They had demons!"

This was yet another haunting that went back a while, like all the way to the 1970's. Rich didn't know the family personally, but he had gone to school with the two boys who'd lived there. He'd listened to the stories his schoolmates were telling, and was undoubtedly sympathetic to their plight. West Street also had stuff going on that was hard to explain. He didn't remember any of the specifics about what was said when I asked him about it forty-plus years later, but it had definitely left an impression on him. He did remember that the family had been forced to leave their house on two separate occasions due to the intensity of the supernatural activity taking place in the home. And he also remembered the name of the classmate who'd shared the stories with him. His name was Scott.

So now I had four different haunted locations on my radar. My grandmother's place and the house next door, the Conjuring House, and the one on Chesley Street. If I considered my cousin's house and my grandmother's house to be a related haunting (and I did), and the Conjuring House to be unrelated because it was almost nine miles away, that only left Chesley Street. That meant that there were only two hauntings in town. And two does not make a pattern. It was certainly a weird coincidence, but not significant as far as I was concerned. It was not until I spoke with Julie and her son LJ that I realized how wrong I'd been. Not only was the Conjuring House related to West Street and Chesley street, it was the known terminus to a freaking ghost hotbed that seemed to involve the entire center of the town of Millville, from Kempton Road to Chestnut Hill and down to Main, up Central and including Ironstone Street, West Street, Hope Street, The Lock, Chesley Street, Quaker Street, Providence Street, Albion, Miller and beyond, possibly all the way to Harrisville itself. It was obvious to me at that point that I was going to need to double back to the house that had reputedly been "infested" with demons. But how was I going to find anyone who remembered anything about it? The haunting had occurred more than forty-five years earlier, and the family had long since moved away. Some of them weren't even still alive.

Taking the family's last name, I first tried to find Scott through social media, but that turned out to be a dead end. Then I tried to cross reference the family name to the street, and *bingo!* Now I knew which house it was, courtesy of an old property tax reference that I found on-line. I also learned who the father was, and that he had passed away in 2016. While searching for the father on social media, I then found an ex-wife of one of the brothers, but the information was old and I couldn't figure out how to contact her. It seemed like a dead end, and it looked like I might never figure out exactly what had taken place in the demon house on Chesley Street. Out of desperation, I posted on the Facebook page *Millville Matters,* asking for help, and I got a hit. Several hits, actually.

Turns out, Gwen and her siblings had been friends with Scott and his Chesley Street family back in the day.

"There was a family that lived in a small house on Chesley Street," she said. "My brother was friends with the son who was his age, we all were, but he would sleep over at their house from time to time."

"Are we talking about the same family?" I inquired, giving her the last name that I had gotten from Richard.

"Yes, that's them. They were just a normal, hard working family. The mother was lovely."

"Can you tell me anything about what happened there?" I asked.

"It was pretty innocuous at first," replied Gwen. "Then it gradually got more violent, until the family finally had to move away. They considered the entities to be something like Laurel and Hardy at first (the slapstick comedy duo from Hollywood's Golden Age of cinema), one was fat and one was skinny. At first it was just like hands coming through the walls and stuff. But then it got physical. My brother finally stopped going over there because he saw them, and he knew that they were not good."

"What did the violence entail?" I asked.

"I will have to ask my brother, he saw them. I know that it escalated and that he has some pretty intense stories. But that's all that I know."

Unfortunately, that's as far as I got in my attempt to uncover that part of the story. Despite reaching out to Gwen again, after being put on radio silence, I never heard back from her or her brother. It's possible that the brother, like so many others that I tried to interview, didn't want to talk about it. Gwen was also supposed to get back to me with details about a farmhouse on Quaker Street that her other brother had previously lived in. It was so haunted that her brother had asked their mom to move in with him. But I obviously didn't get to hear that one either. It is however worth mentioning as an aside, because it brings Quaker Street into the mix as well.

Back to the demon house, out of desperation I took a stab at reaching out to the ex sister-in-law using the only bit of contact information that I had, that being an old Facebook account, but that too went nowhere. Luckily, I got a hit on social media from two other women who had some familiarity with the haunting, otherwise the story may have ended there.

Donna told me that she had been the kids' babysitter back in the 1970's, and that she'd been warned ahead of time about the peculiar living arrangement.

"The mom told me that the home was haunted by a poltergeist," she remembered. "And I believed it. I got very scared there a couple of times."

After a round of banter and some back and forth, it was determined that Donna and her sister Mary may have crossed paths with some of the Smyths back in the day. At the very least, sister Mary had delivered newspapers to my grandfather's estate at 83 Central. But I hadn't come for the small talk.

"Do you remember what creeped you out about the house on Chesley Street?" I asked.

"I was never able to put my finger on it," said Donna. "But the hair on the back of my neck stood up a couple of times. Once, I was spooked while watching TV with the kids. I froze. I asked my twin to come over right away, which he did with several of his friends. They took a look around, but they didn't find anything. Everyone said that I was just afraid because I'd been told that there was a ghost in the house."

Carol had also heard a few stories about the house on Chesley Street. She was the other person who reached out to me. Back in the early part of the 1970's, the Chesley Street address was a place where her husband, cousin, and that cousin's husband would occasionally all pop in for a visit.

"I forget the name of the people who lived there (I was able to confirm that it was the right house and family), but I was told that one night while they were there visiting, the cupboards opened up and all of the dishes started flying off the shelves."

A third contact, who asked not to be identified, confirmed what Gwen had told me about hands coming through the walls, only with added insight into the violence that followed the manifestation. On one occasion, as one of the children was sitting on his bed, a hand came through the wall, grabbed him and proceeded to "beat the shit out of him."

"I thought he was making it up," I was told, "like maybe the parents were doing it. But my brother was there and saw it for himself. He used to sleep over all the time, but he stopped going over there because he got assaulted too."

Unfortunately, that's as far as I got. Thanks to some help by a couple of Facebook sleuths, I got a name and updated contact information for one of the brothers who had grown up in the house. I reached out for an interview, but as had happened to me so many times, it went nowhere. I didn't get a response. I also reached out to a nephew of the family and as a last resort tried to get a message through by asking friends of friends of the family to pass a message along for me. None of it worked. It's too bad too, because there is probably one hell of a story there that isn't getting told. Maybe someday.

# Chapter 24: Monkeying Around In Millville

Going out on a limb here in the believability department, and I wasn't going to include it for a lot of reasons. Primary to my concerns was the fact that this particular story falls outside the box of what I was writing about. It's not a ghost story, and that's what this book is ultimately supposed to be about. Ghost stories, hauntings and encounters with the supernatural to be exact. And that's not what this is. Sure, I'd already gone off the reservation once. I mean, this book was really just supposed to be a story about a haunted house, as in *one* specific haunted house in particular, sitting over on West Street. The same one that my grandmother used to own. I wasn't intending to write a whole story about the dozens of hauntings occurring between Main Street in Millville and the Conjuring House, nine miles away. For one thing, I didn't even know that there were other hauntings in town when I jotted down the first drafts of the first few chapters. It just turned out that way.

The other thing holding me back was the fact that as an adult, I have only mentioned this particular story a few times to a very select number of people that I trust enough to share it with. Why? Because nobody (and I mean *Nobody!*) has ever believed it. And I don't  blame anyone for their skepticism. I wouldn't believe it had I not been there and seen it for myself, because it still makes no sense to me. But it happened, and it happened on West Street. So in a way, it does loosely tie in with the overall theme of what I'm writing about. And it's an interesting story. Fascinating to think about, really. But at some point, I had to wonder if I was risking my credibility by asking people to believe too much. So that's why I wasn't going to mention it. And then Lori reached out to me and I changed my mind.

As the story was related to me, on a summer's evening back in 2006, Lori and a friend were driving down Main Street in Millville, following from behind as their children rode their bikes up by the cemetery, when they encountered what they later believed to have been a pukwudgie.

A pukwudgie is a supernatural creature of Wampanoag folklore said to be half-human and half-goblin. They were described as standing two and a half to three feet tall, having human-like features but with a larger nose, bigger ears and longer fingers. The creatures, which seemed to be a Native American take on the leprechaun, walked on two legs and were covered with thick hair which resembled a porcupine from the back. Legend has it that they were once friendly to people, but later turned against them, subjecting humans to nasty tricks and other forms of harassment once annoyed. Again, sounds familiar to the traits, manners and characteristics common to the legends of folklore found in cultures spread throughout the world. But that's not where I'm going with this. I don't believe in folklore and I wouldn't write a story about it because at the end of the day, I'm only interested in things that actually exist and have actually happened. So why am I including it then? Because I think that Lori is mistaken about what she saw, and I think that what she did see is related to what my brother and I encountered one summer morning back on West Street, as we sat in my grandmother's kitchen eating breakfast. But before we get into that story, let's first go over what Lori and her friend saw on Main Street, and then double back to see how that might tie into what happened to me and my brother nearly thirty years earlier. This is what Lori had to say about that encounter:

"Our young sons were riding their bikes to Cumberland Farms for the first time," she said. "It was getting to be dusk outside, so to preserve this new feeling of independence that they had, we secretly trailed them from way behind as they rode home. When we got to the cemetery, a small creature that we both described as being half-monkey, half-boy ran out from the cemetery and into the road, causing me to slam on my brakes. The monkey-boy stopped and looked at us, then continued running in the direction of the woods, across from the cemetery. We were both in shock. We just looked at each other like, *what the heck was that?* Years later, my husband and I went to the library to attend a presentation on supernatural occurrences, and that was the first time that I realized that what we had seen was a pukwudgie."

"Was it bipedal or walking on its knuckles?" I wondered.

"It was walking on two legs," said Lori. "About two and a half feet tall, with dark hair all over except for the face, which looked to be monkey-ish and human boy-like at the same time."

"What did it look like?" I asked. "Did the head run seamlessly into the shoulders? What can you tell me about the eyes, nose and teeth? I specifically want to know what the nose looked like," I stressed.

"We both mostly remember the big eyes looking back at us," replied Lori. "It had no neck to speak of, like it was hunched over."

As soon as she gave me this description, I had an *ah-ha moment.* This ain't no pukwudgie. That was probably a juvenile. Then I was like, *Holy smokes! A juvenile? Does this mean that they've lived in the woods of Millville this whole time?*

Let me explain.

In February of 1977, a docu-drama began making the rounds in movie theaters across the country by the title of *Sasquatch: The Legend of Bigfoot.* Bigfoot was a hot commodity in the 1970's, perhaps as a result of the Patterson-Gimlin 8mm film, shot along Bluff creek in California back in 1967. Owing to this new found popularity, the cryptid of legend and folklore was making appearances in all kinds of popular television shows of the day, such as *in Search of...*, *The Six Million Dollar Man,* and the Saturday morning series *Bigfoot and Wildboy.* I myself had gone to see the docu-drama during a Saturday matinee one afternoon. Like many investigative shows of that era, the docu-drama re-enacted famous Bigfoot stories, such as the Ape Canyon attack of 1924, in which a group of miners, working in the shadows of MT. Saint Helens had their cabin savagely attacked by a group of "ape-like men," who rained down a hail of large stones upon the roof of the structure one night as the frightened men cowered inside. What set it apart from other media treatments of the day was that the docu-drama claimed to use recordings of real Bigfoot sounds in the filming of their re-enactments.

Fast forward four months to June of 1977 and I'm back on West Street visiting with family, along with my younger brother, sister and mother. I'd been relegated to sleeping on the sofa of the second floor apartment living room on this particular trip north, and that's where I was one early morning when I woke up to a strange sound emanating from out behind the house. It was a long, drawn out wailing type cry. Taken on its own merit, it would have been a strange thing to hear in and of itself. The problem for me was that I immediately recognized what I was hearing. It was an octave for octave, pitch perfect duplication of something that I'd heard in the docu-drama, just a few months earlier. It was an exact replication of what the film had identified as Bigfoot's mating call. And it was coming from the woods out behind my grandmother's house, somewhere to the right and up beyond the grand trunk. [If it interests you, you can hear it for yourself. The last time that I checked, you could still watch the docu-drama for free on YouTube.] For several minutes I lay there on the couch listening to it, spaced out two to five minutes between each call. Nobody else seemed to be awake. I looked at the clock, it was 05:30. Rising from the couch, I moved to the dining room and took a look outside. The dining room windows overlooked the parking area and the backyard. Behind that was a tree line, the old Boston-Hartford rail bed, a culvert, an open field rising up a hill into the grand trunk, and then woods. I didn't see anything, so I went downstairs to my grandmother's apartment. Of course, she was awake.

"Do you hear that?" I asked.

"Oh, it's just dogs up in the hills, howling," she said.

*Dogs?* I thought to myself. *I've never heard a dog make that kind of noise before.*

My grandmother. She seemed to have a ready made excuse for everything, whether it was canines inventing new sounds or water falling over an imaginary dam and making the house rumble. It didn't make sense, but I was open to the possibility. What else could it be? After that, I laid down on my grandmother's couch and listened to it for another twenty minutes or so, until it stopped altogether at about five minutes past six.

By eight thirty in the morning, the house was awake and alive with activity. I had completely forgotten about my early morning wake up call, as I sat at the kitchen table with my younger brother, eating a bowl of cereal. Out of sight, out of mind as it were. My grandmother had a small kitchen. Inside that small kitchen was an aluminum table with a formica top which undoubtedly dated to the early 1960's and was complimentary to the amount of space available to it. It was pressed against the outer kitchen wall and centered beneath two windows which were covered with sheer curtains. I can still remember looking down at my bowl as I stuffed my face. But for some reason, I turned to the right to look at my brother. Then I stopped eating. I was both perplexed and confused by the look on his face. His complexion had gone red and he seemed frozen in the moment, with his eyes bugged out and his mouth hanging open as he looked out the window. His spoon still hung over the bowl, with cereal in the middle and milk dripping from the side of it. Then I turned to see what he was looking at, and I understood what had caused him to do that.

Standing in front of the right kitchen window, filling it entirely with its massive frame and casting a silhouette against the sheer curtain covering the glass, was the thing that I'd heard making all that noise only a few hours earlier. I only had a few seconds to take it in before a loud, powerful and angry growl stood the hair up on the back of my neck, chilled my skin to goose flesh and immediately set my legs in motion as I spun out of my chair and ran for the safety of the living room. As I did that, my brother grimaced and ducked to the left. He would later tell me that he thought that it was going to come through the window. He'd had trouble getting out of his seat, because the open kitchen door behind him blocked him from pushing his seat back far enough to quickly exit the table. Once he got free, he trailed me into the living room as we both shouted *we just saw Bigfoot, we just saw Bigfoot!*

I'm sure you already know what I'm going to say next. Sitting in her chair and watching TV, with a ready-made excuse in hand was my grandmother.

"Oh, someone's just playing a trick on you," she said.

I tried to argue it, but it was pointless. She didn't believe it. In fact, I don't think that anybody ever believed us. My older brother Al had flatly stated that he thought we were lying about it. But here's the thing, for my whole life, if you try telling me that I'm wrong when I know that I'm right, I will do everything in my power to prove to you that it is so. But how do you prove to someone that you've just seen Bigfoot? It clearly wasn't going to be as easy as proving to people that I saw an octopus would be a few years later. I couldn't just wait in the woods and snap a picture of it (and I wouldn't want to!). But what about footprints? Surely it had left footprints. I mean, it always does on TV.

Determined to prove that we weren't lying about what we had seen, I went out past the tree line to look for footprints in the dirt bed of the old railroad track. I didn't find anything, and then it dawned on me, standing a few hundred feet from the house, that the thing might still be in the area. I realized that I was being stupid and ran back to the house. Turns out, I would never be able to prove anything. But what was I trying to prove?

From my perspective on the far side of the kitchen table, looking across the surface of it to the window with the sheer curtain pulled across it, I had seen a large silhouette with a huge head sitting on top of massive shoulders, with no apparent neck. The shoulders were turned out like a man, or a bipedal animal. I hadn't been privy to seeing any details other than that because the curtain was blocking my view. But my brother, who was sitting in the chair against the wall, could see between the spot where the curtain hung and the window frame itself. He'd gotten a real good look at it. In fact, they were practically face to face. This is what he told me:

"I saw it standing outside the window," he would recall. "It was shuffling and bobbing its head, like it was trying to look past the curtains. Then it saw me looking at it and it got mad. Its lip turned up into a snarl and I saw its teeth. They were big and yellow in color, and it had fangs (canine teeth). The eyes were dark, you couldn't see any white in them. It was completely covered in reddish/orange hair. And it had a black nose, like a dog," he added.

That last detail puzzled me for the longest time. Bigfoot would most likely be a primate, and primate's don't have a nose like a dog. I wondered if he had been mistaken, and then I read an article on Yahoo in 2013 that answered the question once and for all.

"Most people don't know that Bigfoot has a black nose, like a dog. That's how we know if people are lying to us or not when they tell us that they've seen it," said a Bigfoot investigator interviewed for the article.

It was an incredible moment of confirmation for me. My brother had said that very same thing thirty-six years before I read the article. It had a black nose, like a dog. He'd seen it for himself. And that, my friends, is why I found Lori's story of an encounter with a pukwudgie so interesting, and why I wanted to include it in this book.

To be fair, I don't know what ran in front of Lori's car on that summer's evening back in 2006. She saw it, and I did not. But it sure makes me wonder if it had a black nose.

Like a dog.

C hapter 25: West Street Redux

When Nancy reached out to me to say that she had a story to tell about West Street, I mistakenly concluded that she was talking about my grandmother's house. Although she was familiar with the house and recalled with kindness my mom's uncle Harry, she was actually referring to her childhood home, a place sitting further down the road and nestled into a spot where West Street meets up with Snow Street. According to one local historian who spoke with the family back in the day, the house had the distinction of being the oldest on West Street, with a date of build stretching all the way back to 1800. Similar to my grandmother's house, Nancy's family home had additions that reportedly had been repurposed from a much older home that dated back to 1735, as told to her by a neighbor by the name of Johnson.

From the moment they moved in, weird and unusual things would begin happening, with Nancy's mom remembering how handles would rattle and turn as if someone were entering a room, only to have doors open by themselves and reveal the fact that there was no one standing behind them, the pots and pans would rattle beneath the sink, to the accompaniment of the dishes shaking inexplicably in the cupboards above.

"Things got moved around all the time with no explanation," recalled Nancy. "Books would go missing for weeks at a time and then suddenly reappear."

According to Nancy's mom, the spirits had been disagreeable in the years prior to the couple having children, but after firstborn Nancy arrived things settled down, as if the arrival of a child in the house convinced the spirits to behave better.

"I had a calming effect on the ghosts, that's what my mom told me," said Nancy. "There was a man who used to appear in my bedroom. He was older, with white hair and thin in appearance. We would sit and have tea parties together, and he taught me how to play poker. Whenever I got in trouble or had an argument with my mom, I would go to my bedroom and he'd be there with words of encouragement. '*It's alright,*' he'd say to me. '*You'll be fine,*' he used to tell me."

As friendly as the male ghost had been to the young girl, he was unfortunately not the only spirit inhabiting the house, as Nancy recalled how the basement always gave her chills. There seemed to be darker forces at work in the tiny village-colonial that the family was sharing with members of the afterlife.

"My sister and I once got a Ouija board for Christmas or a birthday, something like that," Nancy remembered. *(Editor's Note: A Ouija board is a flat board with letters, numbers and simple responses that is used to communicate with the dead. Not sure that it was the best idea for a gift under the circumstances!)* "One day, we were in the bedroom playing with it. I had a doll sitting on a stand on top of my bureau. It was like this porcelain collectible that someone had given to me, and as we're sitting on the floor with our hands on the heart-shaped game piece, the doll turned its head and looked at us as the indicator slid across the board and spelled *Get Out.* Its eyes were glowing red."

Afraid of the doll from that point forward, Nancy would resist getting rid of it for fear that the spirit would retaliate. It wasn't until she was deep into adulthood that she would find the courage to throw it away. As for the Ouija board, they decided to keep it, but not use it in the house.

"We took it across the street, through the woods, over the rail bed and up the hill to the Grand Trunk to play," said Nancy.

It seemed to the young girls like this would certainly be far enough away from the aggressive energy inhabiting their house to safely use the spirit board without too much consequence. Turns out that they should have left well enough alone. This time it spelled out the words, *"You're Going to Die!"* And as it did so, a tree toppled over not far from where the children were playing. Coincidence or not, that spelled the end for the Ouija board.

"We took it home and burned it after that," said Nancy. "We never played with it again."

Also across the street and a little further up the road was an abandoned house that Nancy and her friends used to visit. Something else that she probably should have avoided

"It's gone now," she said. "But we used to go there to explore. The man who had lived there went crazy. He eventually got sent to a mental institution after he went running naked from his house and down the rail bed towards Central Street. The word was that he had been hearing voices."

Whether those voices were all in his head, as with schizophrenia, or were courtesy of something more paranormal than that is just a guess. But it wasn't too dissimilar from what had happened with my grandfather's night nurse back in the 1950's, who'd gone running and screaming down West Street in the middle of the night, after deciding that she'd had enough of the noises that the house was making.

In any event, Nancy's family home now made for three hauntings on West Street, with the possibility of a fourth and a fifth to consider. As I was researching this book, I also heard rumors regarding the three story Victorian that sat on the other side of the street from my grandmother's place, a property once known as the Charles House. The buzz going around was that the sound of music and ballroom dancing could be heard coming from the unoccupied third floor at times. Some people said that footsteps could be heard in empty places. Multiple sources confirmed to me that the house (which had been built in 1847) had indeed once held a ballroom on the top floor, but it was West Street Brenda (from chapter five), who told me that the woman who owned the property previously had been a dance instructor who years ago had given lessons inside the home. So now I knew what the basis for the claims had been, but I was never able to validate the ghost stories that had come through my feed regarding the old Victorian, either by conversation or text interview with any person who'd actually seen or experienced the phenomenon for themselves. However, given the extent to which similar occurrences have been reported in dozens of locations throughout the surrounding neighborhoods, it gives credence to the veracity of the claim. And if we then consider the possibility of the mad streaker's house being haunted as well, then that would bring the total number of confirmed and suspected hauntings on West Street to five.

C hapter 26: The Arnold Estate

I wasn't going to talk about it originally. I mean, there's already a movie trilogy about the place which was based on the book *House of Darkness, House of Light,* by Andrea Perron, who lived in the house on Round Top Road in Burrillville, Rhode Island, from 1971 until the family moved to Georgia in the summer of 1980. *What can I add to the story and what does it have to do with my grandmother's place on West Street?* I wondered. At first, I thought that it was nothing more than a curious coincidence. And then Richard told me about the demon house on Chesley Street, and Julie told me about the house on Chapel Street in Harrisville, just three short miles away. Then her son LJ told me about multiple hauntings that were happening on Hope Street in Millville and also down on Main. Then the floodgates really opened up, and I learned about hauntings on Ironstone Street, Kempton Road, Preston Street, Chestnut Hill Road, Miller Street and Central Street. I had known about the haunting on West Street for almost fifty years, and for most of that time I believed that it was a stand-alone event. Sure, my cousin's house next door was also haunted, but I always considered that spillover from my grandmother's house. As it turned out, that was naive of me. It was becoming more and more clear to me that what was happening at the Conjuring House, just 8.7 miles away, had lots to do with what was also occurring both on West Street and in numerous nearby locations.

The other thought that biased me against including the Conjuring House in this book was the perception that most people already knew the story. *But did they?* I was surprised by the results when I took an informal poll of people that I knew to find that at least half didn't know what or where the Conjuring House was and had never heard the story. It made me realize that I was taking for granted the flag bearer for all of the hauntings taking place in the area. There were movies and books about the old Arnold Estate. But precious few people knew that the very same things were happening on West Street, Hope Street, Chesley Street, Main Street, Chapel Street, at the Lock and numerous other locations over in nearby Millville. I realized that I would be doing the entire story an injustice if I didn't cover at least some of the details regarding the most famous haunted location in the area.

The process by which the Arnold Estate evolved into the Conjuring House began in 1736 when the Richardson family was deeded more than one-thousand acres of land in what is now Burrillville, Rhode Island. Exactly one-hundred years earlier, in 1636, Roger Williams had founded Providence Plantations after being expelled by the Puritan leaders of the Massachusetts Bay Colony for his "erroneous" and "dangerous" opinions. This was a precursor to the Colony of Rhode Island, and later the state of the same name. Williams himself was an English-born Puritan minister and theologian, who was known for his fair dealings with Native Americans. He befriended the great Narragansett chief Canonicus, who first provided refuge for the ostracized Williams, and then gave him the land upon which Providence Plantations was founded. Two other tracts of land were later added to the colony for "a few items" of consideration in return for the Sachem's generosity. These became the towns of Portsmouth and Newport. The land upon which the Arnold Estate sits was incorporated in 1639, when Glocester was added to the Providence Plantations colony. Fearing encroachment by the colonies of Massachusetts and Connecticut, Williams determined that the best way to preserve the land that he had been given was to deed out large parcels of property to those who followed him and adhered to his teachings.

Over the course of the passage of time, the estate originally deeded to the Richardson family was sold off in small parcels, piece by piece, down to just the farmhouse and the 8.5 acres of land that accompany it today. The change in name from Richardson to the Arnold Estate comes courtesy of colonial-era laws which prevented women from owning property, resulting in the deed being transferred through marriage from one family to the other. From there, the property passed into the possession of the Butterworth's through marriage, and then the Kenyon's, where it completed eight consecutive generations of ownership dating back to the original deed. The house's history of infamy began in December of 1970 when it was purchased by Roger and Carolyn Perron, who subsequently moved into the fourteen-room farmhouse with their five children in January of 1971. They would be the first to buy the property who did not have a familial tie to the original Richardson-Arnold Estate.

On moving day, it took about five minutes for the house to give up its secrets, according to daughter Andrea, who recounted that she had seen a man dressed in odd clothing (nineteenth-century?) standing in silence just inside the foyer and watching the family as they carried boxes into the house. When she acknowledged the man with a greeting, operating on the thought that he was with the elderly gentleman who was busy moving out at the same time that the family was moving in, he ignored her. Three of her sisters also asked mom Carolyn who the strange man was, before he mysteriously disappeared. Later that day, as the elder Mr. Kenyon was leaving the property, he pulled Roger aside and told him to leave the lights on at night for the sake of the children. Over the next few months, several neighbors would confide in the family that not a night went by when there was not every single light on in the house. It was an inauspicious beginning to a story that would ultimately spin box-office gold in movie theaters around the world, both near and far from the small rural farmhouse and the otherwise inconspicuous town in which it was located. But it was about to get a whole lot more interesting than that.

Right away, Carolyn Perron noticed that strange things were taking place in the new home. It started small, with items either going missing or moving from one place to another with no apparent explanation, specifically noting that the broom would disappear and then show up again in a place where it had not been left before. Three-miles away and thirty-five years later, the "Borrowers" would drive another couple crazy with the same frustration, as Tom's car keys would go missing in a similar fashion over on Chapel Street, only to then be found in a place he had not remembered leaving them, while Linda seemed to be losing her book every time she put it down. Back on Round Top Road, piles of dirt were also appearing out of nowhere on the newly cleaned kitchen floor, right after it had been swept by Carolyn herself. Then she began to hear noises coming from the empty room, as if something was scraping against the kitchen kettle. Upstairs at night, some of the children were being kept awake by a conglomerate of voices whispering and conversing in the shadows. Daughter Cynthia was being tucked into bed every night and kissed on the forehead by someone that she initially thought was her mother. Andrea Perron later recalled that the presence smelled of "fruits and flowers," while their mother smelled like Ivory soap. Several nights would pass before the sisters realized that it was not their mother tucking them in each night. Meanwhile, Roger Perron was experiencing a cold presence behind him that smelled of rotting flesh, every time that he went down to the basement to service the heating system. In the bedrooms, the beds were seen to be levitating above the floor in the company of that same foul odor. Over on West Street, Richard would report some decades later that he himself had walked in on his own levitating bed, hovering above the floor in the master bedroom of that infamous second-floor apartment that started this book off.

By the family's own account, there were at least a dozen spirits haunting the property, including the man who had watched them from the foyer as they moved their things in. Some of these ghosts were benign, and some of them less amenable to the living beings in the house. One particularly unpleasant male entity took to harassing the five Perron girls in ways that Andrea would later refuse to discuss. And yet the worst of these spirits was believed to be a ghost named Bathsheba.

It was the famed paranormal investigator Lorraine Warren who first identified the supposed witch Bathsheba Sherman as the preeminent evil presence in the house, upon visiting the family unexpectedly and without invitation on a night near Halloween in 1973. Sources differ about how the investigation came about, with some claiming that Carolyn herself reached out for help, while the beleaguered mom denied vehemently that she had ever spoken to anybody. The truth seems to lie somewhere in the fact that the house's dirty little secret wasn't much of a secret to anybody but the Perron family prior to moving in. The house had a reputation that preceded the Perron's involvement, and enough people knew it to draw the attention of a small group of student paranormal investigators, who were all enrolled at Rhode Island College at the time. The team leader was a man named Keith Johnson, and he, his twin brother and some of their friends sought out Ed and Lorraine Warren (who happened to be lecturing at RIC that fall semester) after spending one afternoon at the farmhouse. It should be noted that Andrea Perron herself stated that a family friend named Barbara had been responsible for reaching out to the Warrens, but this doesn't explain why Keith Johnson and his team visited the house first.

Ed Warren was a World War II veteran and former police officer who had self-taught himself demonology, while his wife Lorraine claimed to be a medium and clairvoyant who could communicate with the dead. They formed the New England Society for Psychic Research in 1952, the first and oldest ghost hunting group in New England, achieving their greatest acclaim for the 1975 investigation that became the basis for the 1978 movie *The Amityville Horror.* They were the best known paranormal investigators of the twentieth century and set the standard for the television avalanche of ghost hunting shows that would come later.

As soon as Lorraine pointed the finger at Bathsheba, Carolyn

Perron knew exactly who she was talking about. Carolyn had carefully and meticulously researched the background of the house and surrounding area and recorded her findings in a spiral notebook, detailing encounters, events and depictions of the different spirits that the family were seeing. Supposedly, she had also discovered information that detailed numerous tragedies that had taken place on the property over the eight extended generations that the home had been in the care of the Richardson-Arnold family and their descendants. It was said that numerous children had died in a creek on the property, something that was actually not an uncommon occurrence in colonial-era America. One person was said to have been murdered in the house itself, while several people were noted to have hung themselves in the attic. These are all interesting findings, but there is unfortunately no way to verify what Carolyn claimed to have uncovered. Lorraine Warren took the notebook and never gave it back, despite numerous requests for its return. Despite this, Bathsheba Sherman had indeed been a real person, and the Perron family believed that it was her spirit that was behind the worst of the mischief taking place on the property.

The real Bathsheba Sherman had never actually lived in the house, despite what Lorraine Warren said. In real life she'd lived a mile away, at the Sherman homestead. Talk of her being a witch who'd cursed the land and a satanist who had supposedly sacrificed her own child to the devil in exchange for eternal youth and beauty seemed to be gross exaggerations driven primarily by jealousy, because she was said to be a beautiful and attractive woman who was a threat to other women's ambitions. At this point in history, being accused of being a witch could have dangerous repercussions. It was a tried and true way to eliminate the competition dating back to at least the Salem witch trials, where one amorous young woman tried to get rid of the wife of one John Proctor by accusing her of witchcraft. Instead, she got John Proctor killed in his wife's place when he tried to defend her. Oops!

For Bathsheba Sherman, her troubles were also sparked by an inquest into the sudden death of her own infant child. An autopsy had reportedly discovered that a needle had been inserted at the base of the child's brain. But this was probably nonsense. For one thing, this autopsy predated modern medicine by a hundred years, so it is more likely than not that this was an inaccurate assessment, since "doctors" at this time in history didn't actually know what the hell they were doing or how anything really worked. Consider the fact that when Abraham Lincoln was shot in 1865, or my own ancestor, James Garfield was shot in 1881, doctors had attempted to find the bullets by inserting their naked fingers into the bullet holes. Anybody know what sepsis is? Also consider that the brain is a soft tissue organ that is entirely encased in bone. Suggesting that Bathsheba Sherman inserted a needle into her baby's brain sounds like a story invented by someone who didn't take anatomy into consideration. Need more proof? This supposed "witch" was afforded a Christian service when she passed away and was buried in a Baptist cemetery. That would not have happened in the nineteenth century had there been any truth to the story whatsoever, in a time when those things were taken way too seriously.

Sherman was never charged with a crime, despite the fact that the movie had her killing her own son during a ritual and then hanging herself from a tree on the property. The ugly reality regarding life in the 1800's was that 30% of children died before their first birthday, and 43% died before the age of five. In fact, of the four children that Sherman gave birth to, two of them died at age three and one at age two. Only her third child, Herbert Leander Sherman, managed to outlive his mother, by a total of seventeen years. Bathsheba herself died of old age, so if she had indeed sacrificed her youngest son to the devil for eternal youth and beauty, then she sure as hell got screwed on that deal! There is some historical evidence to suggest that Bathsheba's husband Judson Sherman did indeed die at the Arnold farmhouse, so that at least might explain how the spirit of Bathsheba ended up there, after her death in 1885. But talk of a witch cursing the land seems to have been nothing more than a convenient plot-line for a movie antagonist that was loosely based on some real life jealousy and hearsay.

**The gravestone of Bathsheba Sherman as it stood in the Harrisville Baptist Cemetery prior to being completely destroyed by vandals who had taken the movie's historical account of her life as fact. You can see in the photo that it had already been vandalized and repaired once. It has since been removed and the grave rests in an unmarked location. Photo by brianz190.**

For the Perron family, things would come to a head with the Warren's involvement in the investigation on the fifth and final trip to the farmhouse. Lorraine had insisted upon conducting a séance, telling Carolyn that she was on the verge of being possessed and that her soul would be lost if they did not proceed with the event immediately. Witnessing the proceedings from a darkened corner, daughter Andrea would later recall how her mother soon began to speak in a strange language and that the chair that her mother was sitting in rose from the floor, before being slung into an adjoining room, rendering mom Carolyn unconscious. Husband Roger threw the Warrens and their team out of the house after that and told them never to return, although they did come back later that night to make sure that Carolyn was okay. Pinned down by financial strain, the family would spend another five years in the house before finally moving to Georgia in June of 1980.

So if an old witch's curse isn't responsible for what was occurring at the Arnold Estate, then what explanation was there for all of the things that were happening to the Perron family? One possible influence can be found embedded in the Facebook feed for the special interest group Greater Rhode Island Roaming. Admittedly, it is debatable how much truth can be gleaned from the pages of a social media site, even one dedicated to something as mainstream and straightforward as a directory to central New England hiking hotspots, but one interesting post brings us back to the woods off Jackson Schoolhouse Road, home to Pascoag's own little ghost girl story.

According to the post, if you hike deep enough into the woods in this area you will eventually stumble onto a set of foundations that represent the remnants of old houses that were once used to shelter and quarantine the town's sick and dying, safely isolated away from the rest of the community and essentially left to die alone. If this is true (and I don't know where the author got that information or how accurate it is), then this means that the woods of Burrillville harbor a long and sordid past history steeped in the sadness, sorrow and the suffering that accompanies terminal illness and the cruel and hopeless reality of impending death. It begs the question:

*Did the multitudes of people spending their last miserable days on earth, in this very location, leave an impression of malevolence on the land itself, akin to the accumulation of bad karma and in much the same way that the bloodstained soil of a battlefield can curse the ground upon which those soldiers died, opening the door and serving as a catalyst for future hauntings?*

*Does suffering on a grand scale curse the spot upon which it happened?*

There is plenty of evidence to suggest that this sort of thing does indeed occur, as there are no shortages on earth of locations loaded with a resume full of doom and gloom, such as haunted prisons, asylums, hospitals, battlefields, nursing homes and the like. And yet, another possibility may involve the occult and satanic rituals not related to the false allegations made against Bathsheba Sherman.

Jae Janikowski is a woman who has spent most of her life living on Round Top Road in Harrisville, literally just down the street from the Conjuring House itself. Back in 2009, several years before the movie was released, she and a high school friend went out driving on a Saturday night to nowhere in particular, eventually turning onto a one-way dirt road.

"It started off paved but it quickly turned into a dirt road," she recalled, referring to Collins Taft Road. "We used to go out there to the Little Round Top fishing area to hang out. The road itself went all the way up into Massachusetts. It's just a bunch of houses and farms way out in the woods, in the middle of nowhere. You wouldn't drive down it for any reason except for if you lived there. One night, when I was in high school, a buddy of mine and I drove out to the pond, and as we're driving down the road we saw people way out ahead of us who looked like they were dressed in all black cloaks. You couldn't see them at first, not until the headlights hit them, and they looked like they were carrying something. There were multiple people spread out, and they were carrying something large."

"Could it have been a body of some kind or a sacrificial altar?" I asked, probing for additional details.

"I don't know," she said. "You couldn't see it because it was wrapped up. But it freaked us out. We just looked at each other, and then I pretty much just put the car into reverse after that and backed the entire way out because it was just a little one-lane dirt road."

While there is no way to know for sure exactly what was transpiring in the woods of Burrillville on that Saturday night back in 2009, there are only so many things that adults dressed up in black robes in the middle of the night and out in the woods do together, and one of those things include satanic rituals and devil worship. Although it may have also been related to some kind of Wiccan ceremony.

"There are a ton of witches in that area," Janokowski told me, referring to the modern pagan, earth-centered religion that encompasses theist, atheist and agnostics, but usually not satanist. Some of these ceremonies and services follow the phases of the moon, so that at least may explain the late night shenanigans. Whatever it was that was happening on that particular night, it's probable that it was not the first time that something like that occurred, and it's even more likely that it wasn't the last time that it happened either. But it doesn't satisfy as an explanation for what is and what has been occurring along the ghost corridor between Millville, Massachusetts and Burrillville, Rhode Island. In her April of 2024 interview with the *Bloody Disgusting* Podcast Network, Andrea Perron offered an explanation for the haunting that not only tied in to what Richard said about West Street, it provided a probable and realistic answer to all of the phenomena that was occurring.

To recap what he said, Richard told me during our interview that he believed that an underground source of water passed beneath the West Street property, as evidenced by the fact that the backyard area used to flood out extensively prior to a drainage system being installed. Water has long been thought to be a conduit for spiritual manifestations. Ground flow water also generates a weak electromagnetic field as it passes through the strata beneath the topsoil, and electromagnetic energy has also been implicated in the occurrence of supernatural activity. According to Perron, a river running deep beneath the property comprising the old Arnold Estate may offer the best explanation for what has been seen to occur there.

"The farm is built on top of an ancient river," said Perron, during her interview with author Michelle Swope. "It's known as the Lost River of New Hampshire, but it actually runs all the way underground. It's buried about 700 feet underground. And on certain days when the water is very heightened and rushing, you can actually feel the vibration of it on the land. And you can lay on the stone walls and feel the stones vibrating from the river rushing underneath our feet. And it goes directly underneath the farm, but also there are two creeks or tributaries to the Nipmuc River, which runs right along the bottom of the property, just beyond the stone wall that marks the backyard." This is just an excerpt from what she had to say about the Arnold Estate. If you would like to read the full interview, please go to:

https://bloody-disgusting.com/interviews/3808398/be-not-afraid-andrea-perron-shares-the-chilling-true-story-behind-the-conjuring-interview/

As it stands today, the Conjuring House operates as a tourist attraction and a money-making operation. It is open for ghost tours, paranormal investigations and a menu of different camping experiences. I originally intended to take my daughter on a tour of the house the summer that I was writing and researching this book, but a spat of bad publicity related to new ownership made me change my mind. Then I was told that I might be able to get into the haunted attic that I talked about on Hope Street, and I totally wrote off a visit to Harrisville. Unfortunately, neither of those things happened. I was not expecting that we would see ghosts on a visit to the Conjuring House, but I know that there is a feeling that you get when you're alone but you're not alone. Whether you can see it or not, spirits give off a distinctive vibe that you can feel. West Street had that feeling, and I was interested to find out if I could pick up on it again. It's a palpable feeling that you get that you're not alone, even when your eyes and ears tell you differently. If you know, then you know. If you've never experienced it personally, then that probably makes no sense to you.

The Conjuring House likes to bill itself as one of the most haunted places in the United States. That's absurd. For one thing, you can't qualify or quantify a claim like that. It's a marketing ploy, plain and simple. The reality is that the whole area running from Main Street Harrisville to Main Street in Millville, Massachusetts is teeming with paranormal activity. On Chapel Street alone, just three miles from the Conjuring Hose, is a three-apartment building housing at least nine different entities. These are just the properties that I know about. I definitely did not uncover everything that is going on along that particular stretch of land. In fact, I'm certain that I only captured some small piece of the overall truth. So in a way the Conjuring House may indeed be one of the most haunted places in America, but that is mostly true only as a part of a much larger story. Most of which you won't see in the movies.

# EPILOGUE

What I find most interesting about those experiences from the attic all these years later, thinking about it from the angle of being a mature, educated and analytically-minded person, is that those spirits that I encountered had somehow failed to move on to the next thing. If you are a religious person, then it begs the question: *Why didn't they go to heaven?* If you believe in transmigration, which is the endless cycle of birth-death-and rebirth, then *Why did they fail to follow the cycle? What separated them from what most people believe is the normal progression of things? Did they not follow the light on purpose? And why would they do that? Is the phenomenon that is obviously taking place on West Street and other nearby locations blocking the light, or just giving spirits the option to stay or move on?*

It is impossible to know. At least in my experience, I never had the chance to ask the ghosts that I encountered why they were there. Not that I would have. Thankfully, they returned to wherever they came from whenever I approached, sinking into the background like a mirage at the distant end of a paved road, baking beneath a hot sun. I never actually saw who was making all that noise in the pool room, and as a kid I was happy that I didn't. It was bad enough just knowing that they were there.

Still it's interesting to note that the ghosts were seeking entertainment, they were talking to each other and laughing about stuff. *What do dead people find so funny, anyway?* Because they were shooting pool, I'm going to assume that they had been familiar with the game when they were alive. *Had they been patrons of the old pool hall down on Main Street? Did they all know each other when they'd been alive*? I only heard male voices in my personal encounters. And what about that? *What the hell do dead people talk about? Do they just talk about the good old days?* Because it isn't girls, sports or current events. None of that should matter to them anymore. And what about the letter that I found? If you want to believe that one of the ghosts left it beneath the chair (and I do), that suggests that it might have once belonged to the reader, who would have been alive 90 something years before this. He'd probably been dead at that point for some time. *Why was he stuck reminiscing about the past? Why else would he be sitting in that chair reading a letter that was almost a hundred years old? Who was he and what was his tie to that particular house? Did he even have one? Or, was that just the portal that he happened to use? Why reminisce about stuff that no longer matters if you have the option to move on?* As I think about it, the name of at least one of those ghosts was probably on that letter. In the greeting perhaps. If I could have read it, I may have gotten the answers to some of those questions. But as it stands, I'll never know.

I don't know anything about the history of that house, other than the people who lived there prior to my cousin purchasing the property in the 1970's were of Swedish ancestry. I don't know if anyone ever died in that house. I don't think that wakes were ever held there, like they were next door. I never had any explanation for why it was haunted, other than the fact that it sat next door to my grandmother's house, which sits on a stretch of land that seems to me to be one of the most haunted places in Massachusetts.

My grandmother's house? Now that was a different story altogether. That haunting may have had a reasonable catalyst behind it. People had specifically died in that house. Wakes had been held there. Is it a coincidence that it isn't very far from the Conjuring House? Or the house on Chapel Street? Or that a house just two streets over was reportedly inhabited by demons? Or that there are two haunted locations on Hope Street and five on Main? Or that the countryside itself is full of reported sightings? Maybe there really is  an underground flow of water running through all of these properties that serves as a conduit that ultimately allows these manifestations to happen, as it flows down from New Hampshire, and possibly mingles with the Blackstone River. Maybe Millville just happens to sit within an electromagnetic hotspot. There are dozens of such places on the surface of the earth where the electromagnetic energy generated at the earth's core are especially strong, such as the Bermuda Triangle, the Alaskan Triangle and the Devil's Sea. Whatever the catalyst, it's clear from the testimonials of so many disparate individuals that something is allowing portals to form not only on West Street, but up and down this ghost corridor running from the Main Street in Millville, all the way down into Rhode Island. One final note, it's a way bigger story than what you've read here. For every person who gave me an interview, there was a multiple of people who didn't want to talk about it. For all I know, the hauntings do not start in Millville, nor do they stop in Burrillville. In fact, I think that's likely.

# Chapter Finis: Other Books By This Author

DONALD SMYTH

THE
ALPHA OF
PURGATORY

When a man living off the grid in the remote Purgatory Valley with a pack of orphaned wolves reluctantly teams up with the head of a conservation effort aimed at restoring the gray wolf population of Yellowstone National Park, they unwittingly become entangled in a violent conspiracy determined to derail the reintroduction plan, beginning with the attempted murder of the plan's administrator.

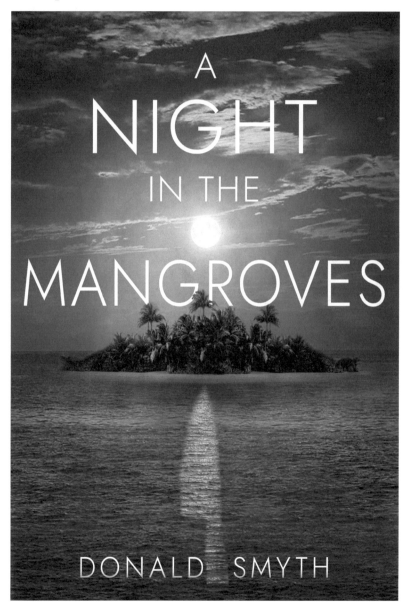

Three young teenage friends go camping on a deserted island sitting off the coast of the Florida Keys, only to find themselves being tormented by an unseen threat as nightfall drops a curtain of darkness over the isolated landscape. Who's stalking the boys and what do they want? That will be the mystery that two detectives will try to unravel forty years later when they are called upon to investigate the discovery of two skeletons found hidden beneath a small, overturned boat in the densely overgrown interior of the private island known as Shands Key.

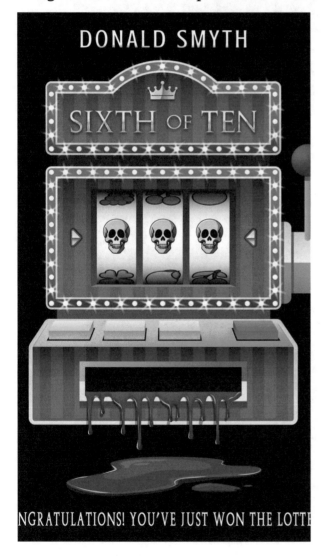

He's just won the lottery, and she's just been assigned to kill him. When a disfigured and narcoleptic teenager wins the annual and onerous State sponsored death lottery, he makes a mad 1,300 mile dash for the border of the nearest country that offers refuge to lottery winners, traveling along a modern Underground Railroad and pursued by his State assigned assassin, who will stop at nothing to expose and destroy the carefully coordinated escape route, while preventing her target from making it to freedom at the same time.

# AFTERWORD

I had no idea what I was getting into when I began writting this book. I thought that I was undertaking a project about a story regarding my grandmother's house on West Street. The real story proved to be way more interesting than that. And unfortunately, it's probably way more interesting than what you've read here. For every interview that I got, there were at least two people that wouldn't return my messages. That was frustrating, and for long stretches at a time I wondered if I would even be able to get enough interviews to finish this book. Little by little, I would get a break here and there until I had finally accumulated enough material to tell a compelling story. Not as it turns out, a story about one particular haunting, but of one giant haunting encompassing the center of an entire town, and stretching down into the northern part of Rhode Isand, including the world-famous Conjuring House itself. Who knew? I certainly didn't. I thought that my grandmother's house was the only haunted house in town. I suspect that the whole truth is even stranger than this, and even more incredible than what you've read here.

Donald Ballou Smyth- February 17, 2025

# ACKNOWLEDGEMENT

I've got some work to do here for a change. As a fiction writer, I had not previously put out a book that depended upon the help and/or assistance of other people. So writting a non-fiction book about a host of varied real-life encounters was a challenge, and I absolutely could not have completed it without the help of a bunch of people. A great big thank you needs to go out to Terri (you know who you are) for being the first person to step up to the plate and give me an interview, when I couldn't get anyone else to talk about it. She's the one who got the ball rolling. If I was giving out gold stars, then Julie Nogler would have to be first in line. She's the one who told me about the Chapel Street haunting and she's also the one who conducted those interviews for me. Not only that, but she also referred me to her son, LJ, who subsequently told me about five other hauntings taking place within walking distance of my grandmother's house. That was the first time that I began to realize the magnitude and the scope of the true story that needed to be told. Special thanks need to go out to L. Clement of the Millville Historical Commission for sharing all of his great photos with me. He was also instrumental in helping me figure out where the bowling alley had been in town and in helping me to unravel the mystery behind the Lucy on the Lock haunting. I had once heard about the Dumas family tragedy, back in the 1970's. But I had totally forgotten about it until it came up during our interview. Last but certainly not least, thank you to all of the great people who live in the town of Millville who were willing to share their stories with me for the purposes of helping me to write this fascinating book. I could not have taken it to publication without your help.

# ABOUT THE AUTHOR

## Donald Ballou Smyth

Donald Ballou Smyth was raised in the Florida Keys and is a graduate of the Animal Science/Pre-Veterinary program at the University of Massachusetts, at Amherst, earning Cum Laude and Commonwealth Scholar honors as a student there in the 1990's. He is an ASCP  certified Medical Technologist working in the field of transfusion medicine at the largest trauma center in central Massachusetts. He is also the author of the wilderness/suspense thriller The Alpha of Purgatory, the young adult murder mystery A Night in the Mangroves, and the dystopian novel Sixth of Ten. He is related through his paternal grandmother to the nineteenth century writer Adin Ballou, whom Leo Tolstoy once called "America's greatest writer."

For news and updates about this and future releases, Follow me at Amazon or on Facebook at:

https://www.facebook.com/TheAlphaofPurgatory

https://amazon.com/author/donald.ballou.smyth

Made in the USA
Columbia, SC
26 April 2025

57179888R00102